Dreams and Wishful Thinking

Kristine Erinn

ISBN: 978-1-7352027-1-6
ISBN: 978-1-7352027-0-9

Cover Art and Design: Sharon Bray
Library of Congress Control Number: 2020911483
Printed in the United States of America

Acknowledgments

This book is such an achievement for me as it is my first published book. So many great minds and hearts have put the effort into making this book something that I can be truly proud of and I can't thank everyone enough.

My friends and family pushed me to do my best and always lent a helping hand when I needed it. I couldn't have gotten this collection out there without all of you.

To my parents, Shelly and Sam, my boyfriend Steven, my grandmother Ann, and my godparents Paula and David, you encouraged me to make my dream come true with this first book. Without you, I could never have accomplished everything that I wanted to in this book.

Also, to all my college friends thank you for helping me edit the book, it's a great relief to have multiple people working together to help me make these stories even better.

Sharon Bray, you are a great artist and I thank you so much for putting the time and effort into the cover art for this book. Without you this beautiful cover would never have made it to my readers.

I would also like to express my gratitude to Professor Shane Borrowman for helping me through this long process and finally getting my senior thesis out there for the world to see.

*"You know what the issue is with this world?
Everyone wants some magical solution to their
problem & everyone refuses to believe in magic."*
~ Lewis Carrol

Contents

Introduction

This collection of short stories has changed from my middle school years up until my graduation from college. These writings have grown from my imagination in such a way that when I first started, I never would have imagined would become what they are today. Many of them started out as class projects, little writing prompts that needed to have vocabulary words or start out of a certain topic, most have some origin that started in my dreams and have become a reality on the page. None-the-less all have a unique angle that I adore creating. These worlds tie influences from mythologies and books that I have discovered over the years.

I've adapted some of the plotlines and characters to fit my modern style, as many authors will tell anyone "what one writes when they are young will not be what they are writing when they are older." I have learned and grown throughout these years and these stories have shown me just how much that is true. But I couldn't let these stories lie the way they were. This collection is a sample of what I love to create. Characters and stories are meant to be shared with the world so they can be enjoyed more than I can give them credit for.

I have shaped my worlds with names that mean something. Most of the characters in this work have names with fascinating meanings. The names of the characters are chosen because of a meaning that ties it to the personality of the character or an essential theme to the story itself. I love the idea of having a meaning to a character and I think I will continue that same theme for the rest of my career.

Dreams shape my reality when writing. The beautiful images that have flashed in my head every night made myths of my own. Dreams are the most important thing to me as an author. I draw much inspiration from my subconscious and from the world around me. If anything, I would love for my readers to take inspiration from these stories and create their own worlds.

Collective Short Stories

Reluctant Brothers

I wrote this during my very first year of college for a final assignment in sociology class. I was never one for doing research papers and my professor allowed me to try something where my talent shined the most. The picture I drew to accompany this story is Liam's family picture that is referenced many times within the story. I have always loved history and the World Wars; this piece is about the first World War which hung a heavy burden on my heart as I have read many stories about the men and woman who lost their lives in such tragedy. Thus, I put my hopes, fears, and sadness into this piece. ~ K. E.

I was nothing like anyone wanted and everything everyone expected. Some called me the universal soldier, others said I was nothing but the new guy. I wasn't so new anymore; I had been stationed on the border of France and Germany for two months now. I saw things and had killed people.

Positioned in the trenches, I fired at the German forces. We had not advanced in the slightest but neither had they. The old soldiers, the ones who had survived here the longest, were tired of this war. The newer recruits began to realize that the war was a politician's game. They kept telling us we were winning, that everything would be fine. We knew that was a lie.

People could tell us what the war was about, safety, protection of the country, and land disputes. We heard everything. It was not about that at all, not to us. We had to kill them, and they had to kill us. We knew nothing more than that. It was not a kill or be killed war. No, it was a kill now, die later war.

We wanted to go home. I would say that even the Germans wanted to go home. But every day I watched men on both fronts drop dead, some from bullet wounds, others from disease. We had limited medical supplies. Our living conditions were strained. It was a living hell of nothingness.

The mission I remember out of the entire war, was a time I will never forget. I woke to the sound of cannons that spring... I think it was spring, morning. The gun and cannon fire filled the air and shook the ground. I had gotten used to sleeping with these sounds all around me. The smells of rotting fluids filled the air, mixing with the fiery scent of gunpowder. The world looked dull, grey, and lifeless, not counting some of the bodies of the freshly dead men that lay with eyes open.

Nothing was different: every smell, sight, and sound was the same as the day before. Everything was the same ... even me. I was still caked with mud and filth. My red hair was as brown as the small farming roads of home... Home...I shook myself awake and looked around for any ration crates. Any food at all would be wonderful.

Again, nothing. There was nothing here for us, nothing there for them. We were fighting a war that was not our own and the only emotions we knew were fear, sadness, and anger. If you asked anyone on either side, why they felt that way, they could probably never tell you the full truth.

I groaned, raising my gun up to reload it. 'No food, just fire.' I told myself. Once the gun was ready, I began firing at the enemy, peeking my head up just enough to take aim and fire. I had hardly any commitment anymore and I didn't even feel like I was human.

I shot only a handful of men within a few hours. I myself was lucky enough to dodge several bullets that came my way. One came within inches of my head, piercing my cap instead. The shooter gave me one small glance before I scrambled down, taking my cap off quickly. Desperately, I swept my fingers around trying to find the photo hidden within the rim. I held it up a bit to see my mother, father, sister, and I standing at a parade, long ago at least when I was nineteen. My darling sister raised the Irish flag in pride while we all smiled. Only the corner of the photo was taken off. I breathed a sigh of relief and placed it back in my cap.

I sat there for a while pondering my emotions. The only thing I cared about was at home and in my cap. I adjusted my hat just the way dad had. My hands twitched in frustration. This war, this war needed to end. My eyes closed as my hands balled into fists. I could see home, the emerald green fields with my parent's small house standing tall with the smoke tumbling out of the chimney.

The smell of lamb cooking in the pot seeped out of every nook and cranny. My mum's humming of one of the oldest tunes she knew swam around in my head. I could never name the song, but I could sing every note as she did. Aine, my little sister, ran out to hug me with all the joy in the world.

"Sing what mum's humming! Please, Liam, please!" she whined, throwing her arms around my neck.

"Sure Aine, course I'll sing for ya." I began to sing for her in my deep smooth voice that put many church choir men to shame.

Then I heard it, a name called out, my name. I opened my eyes to find the Major coming my way yelling. I didn't think he even knew my name. I sure didn't know his. He was British dirt.

"Liam, you shut your mouth with that bloody singing! You got a new job; get your things, you're heading out to get a hold of a German surreptitious operation." I quit my singing, which I hadn't realized I was doing. I wanted to scream at the Brit to tell him to speak English, but I held my tongue. He must have read the dictionary every night rather than a Bible, because he always used such ridiculous big words.

"What's the mission sir?" I slid down the trench a bit to stand up fully so I wouldn't get shot and saluted him.

"Didn't you hear me?! You're going to take out some Germans. They're planning to sneak behind our lines through an old desolated French town. The Lieutenant and his men are taking a tank and you will be one of the ground troops escorting it. Now go and don't make them wait." He pointed me in the direction he had come, then quickly marched down the trench, probably to go pick on another poor Irish chap. I huffed, loosened my stance and looked around for anything I may have had. Nothing.

"Alright then." I shoved off, grabbing the filthy grimy jacket I laid on. Slinging my gun over my shoulder and tossing the jacket over the gun, I started to sing mum's song once more.

I didn't expect the few foot soldiers that were going on the mission. There were five of us in total that traveled alongside the tank. It took us a good day or so to come to the location and by then I was thoroughly upset. I cussed out my fellow British and French companions several times. Finally, I resorted to cussing in Gaelic for so they wouldn't understand.

It was silent when we reached the outskirts of the city ruins. Not a living thing could be seen; the buildings were filled with ruble and collapsing. I moved to the outer part of our circle near the buildings. Then there was a bright light. I was knocked off my feet; my body thrown into the alley, hitting one exterior wall. The sound was deafening, leaving pounding as much as if it were a beating drum in my head.

It was so quiet now, so dark. My heart skipped before I could no longer think.

The darkness was overwhelming. I felt suffocated and scared. 'So, this is death.' I thought, I was prepared for my own death but now I couldn't help but to shake in fear. I thought it would be lonely though. I didn't feel alone here in this darkness. What was this?

I felt a sharp pain at my side, well what I thought was my side. My eyes shot open. My body lurched forward into what seemed to be a sitting position. I groaned in pain as the light and darkness blurred. A gentle hand pushed me back to lay down.

"Easy, that blast almost killed you." The voice that spoke to me was gruff, definitely male. He wasn't British…or any ally I had heard of. His voice was different. I panicked finally recognizing the accent.

"Get away from me, you filthy German!" I screamed at the top of my lungs, pulling to the side away from him. My back slammed against a wall as I tried to swing with my right hand, but it was restrained. He was a blur but slightly larger than me.

"That's no way to treat a man who saved your life." I felt lightheaded and waited for him to shoot me. The bullet never came. His words sunk in.

"You saved me?" my vision began to focus on a strong-jawed man who looked only a few years older than me, if that. He was a bit grimy like me, but his blue eyes and blond hair stood out through the dirt. Typical German.

"Yes, I did. Really, you were lucky. You were far enough away that you weren't killed." He sat there, unmoving.

"Why wouldn't you let me die?" I held my right arm gently. It was broken.

"Don't move. Your arms broken in two places. Your heads bandaged too, so don't touch it." He sat back in his chair, watching me. I rubbed my arm gently.

"What about the rest of the men I was with?" I knew the answer, but I needed to hear it said out loud.

"Dead. My platoon checked. I found you and decided to come back to help you."

"Why? Why would you save me?" Our eyes met and for a second, we were the same. Not German. Not Irish. We were just men.

"I was going to kill you but," he paused taking out a small picture from his jacket. My eyes went wide, "this was a little ways away from you. It's your family, right?"

I nodded, shocked as he handed it back to me. My thumb trailed over the figures once it touched my hand. He then grabbed out a small picture of his own. He turned it so I could see.

"I have one of my own. Not as large as yours, I was an only child. You're like me when it comes to family, I guess." He tucked the picture back into his coat.

"I suppose we are. We're different in everything else though. You look like a rich boy and you're German."

"I suppose I am, but we're both in this war, aren't we?" I nodded thinking about it again. The German smiled and nodded as if to say you're a man, I'm a man, we're just surviving. "My name's Otho. What's yours, Irishman?"

"Name's Liam."

Otho was a nice German. No, not German, a man. He was twenty-three, that made him two years older than me. He talked about how he was from a richer class and signed up to become a soldier when his father pressured him. He explained that it was all about honor for his father. Otho wanted to please him, wanted him to look at his son as a strong protector ready to take on the world.

That wasn't the case, though. Otho wanted to go home; he was as tired of this war as I was. We connected, oddly enough. A poor Irish boy understood a rich German lad. We spent a night together in that old rundown building where he nursed my wounds. We did nothing but talk about how the war was nothing to us, how we missed home and how we would change the world when we got back.

We had the same lust for peace, and I couldn't help but feel like he was my own brother. We even drank some wine that we'd found in the building, then complained how we wanted something stronger like beer or whiskey. That day was the best day I had experienced, except for the day I went home.

We parted our ways the next morning. He went back to his regiment; I went back to mine. I watched him as he left me, sad to see him leave. I knew what would happen to him and it was like I was losing one of my own family.

I was one of the lucky ones that survived the war. I went back home with my arm still broken and new scrapes and cuts. My mother fussed over me for weeks, cussing the British in Gaelic. When the Irish revolution hit, I helped, risking my life many more times.

It wasn't until years later when I had a family of my own that I thought about finding my brother Otho. I took my family on a vacation to Germany one winter. Without their knowledge I snuck out to go find records about his family. I ended up finding his family in an old newspaper. He died in the war from the shot of a tank. His mother died shortly after; I suppose from a broken heart. His father committed suicide after both his son and wife were dead.

I spent a long time in those records, weeping for my lost brother. If only the war had never happened, both he and I would be alive. Two brothers separated by a world of hate, injustice, deceit, and pain. If only the Great War wouldn't have happened.

The White stag and the Night

This piece was created in Highschool for another Creative Writing assignment. The white stag has always been an interesting mythological creature that I have been drawn too, especially since I loved J.K. Rowling's patronus charms for Harry and James. They aren't the same thing but they both have an elegance that only a white deer can hold. ~ K.E.

Once, long ago before man had taken the forests the White Stag roamed the land nobly ruling all. He kept watch over the sun filled land. His mighty antlers made the mighty king stand out above all and would shine brightly in the suns glorious light. But as time dragged on, he noticed all the animals, all the people, and even all of the plants grew very weary for they could not sleep with the suns ever vivid light shining into their eyes.

The mighty White Stag decided to do something about this problem. He wandered across the earth and noticed the shadows. They did not move, and they even looked tired. Along a rocky cliff side, he stopped and talked to a shadow hiding behind a rock. "Why are you so tired little shadow?" The great White Stag asked.

"There is no darkness but that which is here. I cannot run to find new shelter. I cannot do anything because there is no darkness besides myself." The White Stag looked at the cowering little shadow.

"Darkness you say?" he looked up at the sky wondering what he could do. He then thought about something his friend Red Dragon had once said. He knew in that moment that he must go visit Red Dragon to hear the story once more.

The White Stag did not have to travel far before he came across the cave of the Red Dragon. It was the only cave on the earth, Red Dragon had spent much time making it for himself. The White Stag hesitantly entered the long cavern. He went back very far, far enough that the sun no longer shown. The darkness was very strange for him. It was hard for him to walk anywhere without tripping, but Red Dragon's cave was very clean and well made. After quite some time in the darkness he began to feel very sleepy. He soon decided that Red Dragon would not mind if he closed his eyes for just a bit.

The White Stag soon awoke to the gentle hum of an ancient song. He opened his eyes to see that the Red Dragon had lit a fire and was sitting behind it watching White Stag. "Dear Stag, you have finally found rest within the darkness. How was your gentle sleep?"

The White Stag jumped up startled. "Sleep? Was I asleep? How long was I asleep?" He looked around quickly forgetting that he was in a cave.

"Dear White Stag you were asleep for 3 days." Stag looked confused. Days? What were days? Red Dragon looked down to him smiling.

"Yes, dear friend days. The reason why you came to see me. The story I long ago told you of a land far beyond the Sun. Darkness would descend upon the land and then the Sun would come back again. That is why I made this cave so I could sleep in darkness and awake to go out into the sun. The land is not far beyond the sun in the sky." White Stag looked up to his old friend.

"Is that what the land needs? Darkness? The darkness of the land?" Red Dragon looked down concerned.

"No Stag not just darkness. There must be light. Just as I have provided light with this fire there must be light within the sky. The mistress of the darkness could help you if you could seek an audience. Her name is Moon." The White Stag turned back to the darkness.

"I shall do this for the land!" He exclaimed. "I shall let all my subjects rest under what shall be known as night." The White Stag then immediately dashed out of Red Dragons cave quickly running for the tallest mountain. He reached the top and began to look into the sky.

"Moon! Dear mistress Moon!" He cried out. For hours upon hours he called out to Mistress

15

Moon with no answer. The White Stag became weary and losing faith shed tears for his people knowing that they would never find the peace of sleep.

The Sun saw the pain and heartache of the creature and decided to let his sister talk to the poor White Stag. Sun moved back out of the sky, his sister came out from behind him. Moon crept into the sky letting darkness fall upon the land. She looked down upon the White Stag who glanced up to meet the great mistress.

"Poor dear White Stag why do you weep?" The White Stag jumped up quickly greeting the Moon.

"Mistress Moon! Please help my dear people. Your brother Sun shines so bright that the world cannot sleep!" Moon shone her light on the White Stag so that his fur glowed bright. She raised his tears into the sky making all of them into stars.

"My dear White Stag I shall bring the night to you every day. I shall share the sky with my brother and allow the world to rest under my watchful care. Your tears shall shine bright beside me to tell the world how much you care for it." The White Stag was joyful. Every day Moon and Sun shared the sky giving sleep and awareness to the world. White Stag watched over the land and thanked both Sun and Moon every time one appeared in the sky.

Creation

When I started this creation story. I didn't have a plan. This was from my Highschool Creative Writing class and I just started with a small concept and expanded outwards. Creation stories have always fascinated me, so it was interesting and satisfying to create one of my own. ~ K.E.

Long ago when there was nothing but black and white floating in the middle of the vast nothingness, something stirred within the void. It started to move and twist and spread. It soon became the shape of a young woman with white skin, black hair, fluffy ears, and a black and white tail. She looked at herself with her white eyes and slowly began to see that the white mixed and formed into colors. Her skin slowly turned a light peach; her cheeks and lips became red. Her eyes began to mirror all the colors that we now know. As she looked around the vast nothingness, she felt very alone.

She decided to see if colors could form around her. She decided she would make others like her to keep her company. She breathed into the air blue smoke which danced, expanded, and created the sky. She stomped her feet and bright greens and deep rich browns rumbled across the expanse making the ground. She danced along the new earth leaving footprints of growing flowers, shrubs, trees, and vines. She opened her mouth as two bubbles appeared one of bright yellow gold, and the other of a brilliant silvery white which floated into the sky and turned into the sun and moon. She shed tears of happiness as the colors scorched the emptiness and the tears rose becoming the stars. Once again, she was overcome with joy, she howled to the moon. From her howls came the first creatures, the wolves. As she kept singing her song more creatures appeared jumping from her words onto the earth. The last to appear were man and woman.

Overjoyed with her new friends she began to teach each and every one to do what they must to survive on their own. It took man and woman longer than the others to learn and they are still learning. Sometimes they would listen to her, but then they would go on trying to figure out the world on their own. They started to do more things on their own, however wrong they were. The creator tried to help as best she could, but she decided she had done everything she could. She, who stays nameless to this day, flew up to meet the moon, sun, and stars, where she stayed watching over her creation, watching to see how and when they would call for her, if they ever did. When they

did call the creator was pleased. She would des-
cend to be with her friends once more.

The ghost and the Banshee

This story was my early attempt at a love story mixed with a Halloween legend. It was for one of my vocabulary assignments and honestly, I wanted to try my hand at a pure romantic story. It is my older language, but I still believe it is a point of growth for me. ~ K.E.

I will tell you a tale of all Hollows-eve romance. Once, long ago there was a miserable ghost. He wished to tell his history to the family living in the house of his birth. They saw his communication as a threat on their lives. With the seclusion of the ghost based on fear, he babbled to himself and pretended they would listen. He thought long and hard for many years about his current predicament. The more thought he put into it the larger an infernal rage grew within him. The more anger he had the more his battered soul deteriorated. He felt as if he was slowly falling into the abyss in which his human heart feared so much. He finally made a resolute decision to leave the dreaded place of his torment and search for someone who would listen.

He wandered across the land going from town to town with this hope. He searched and searched until one day he came across a village struck with a deadly pestilence. He thought this was like any other place he passed through, but his acute hearing and vigilant eyes detected a lovely creature. The maiden had a morbid tone to her wailing as she walked the streets. The throng of people cowered away from her mournful weeping and vainly threw themselves into their homes and shops thinking they could escape the sound. He hid himself as well but not in fear. She was like him! No one saw her! There was a difference between them though. She could be heard.

He watched her for a good thirty minutes observing her actions and her appearance. She was a woman around the same age as he, with brown curly hair about the length of her mid back. She had blue eyes that were being blurred by her crying. Her skin was pale as if resembling how sad she was. A beautiful dress of forest green and blood red lay on her with an elegance of a royal's gown. She walked the town streets pausing for an instant at many different houses then continued her journey. He contemplated many of his own thoughts and by the time he decided to reveal himself to her, she had gone into the very center of the village. She cried and sobbed with the loudness that resembled thunder in the night sky. He slowly approached her and stopped a few feet away from her turned back.

"Why do you weep in such a manner mi' lady?" He spoke in the softest voice he could manage. She jumped slightly not used to being recognized.

"Why do I weep?" she questioned half dumbfounded, while wiping away tears. She turned and looked at the man who spoke. He had a noble look to him as if he were some knight from the high castles.

"I weep because it is my purpose" she whispered "I must weep for the people who have lost their lives. It is so sad how they die in such ignominious ways."

"But there are many dying here. How can you have peace in such a place?" He was afflicted with such a sad thought that this lovely girl would have to be sad and alone with this much grief. She was not much unlike himself.

"So, I must weep for them all. A ghostly knight like yourself should know that we will not be at peace. We can not, I have tried and failed." She said tears again swelling in her eyes. With an efficacy of sympathy, he spoke sternly but softly.

"We can be at peace for we are no longer alone. We can help one another and scourge this sadness from our hearts."

"I will listen to you knight for you have a hope in your eyes of the likes I have never seen. Such hope should be kindled. Now, pray tell me why you are as sad as I?"

She showed a small pure smile and started

walking towards the forest in whence he had first arrived. He kept pace with her and told her that once he was a Knight who was factored by the king. When the king became corrupt, the Knight acted contumaciously and was killed for his defiance. He felt lighter as he told the story. Though his story was sad he had a small smile, for the maiden at his side was in awe of him.

"How brave you are Sir Knight!" she exclaimed "If only I was as good a creature as you!"

"You are better than me in every way, you cannot be less than a priestess." He smiled a bit flirtatiously.

"I am a banshee kind sir nothing to be adorned with such words that you speak." She blushed out of shame and flattery.

"A young maiden such as you can only be as pure as snow, no matter what you call yourself. Now then would you be so kind as to join me on a walk on this lovely Hollows-eve mi' Lady?" He put up his arm ready to receive hers.

"Why of course my honorable Knight. Let us enjoy the night." She took up his arm, both with the hope to find peace with each other. They disappeared into the forest.

Now it is said that these two spirits soon became lovers and if you are lucky enough you will see a glimpse of the two holding hands along the forests edge on Hollows-eve.

Moonlight

Moonlight was also an assignment from my earlier years. I have always loved going outside and looking up at the moon. The feeling that comes with those awe-inspiring moments is what created this tale. I tried to capture my emotions and feelings within these words. ~ K.E.

The moon so bright, so cold, and welcoming. Its motherly care looks over the land protecting all it sees. Every night she watches over all the creatures, wishing and praying the creatures live happily surrounded in her brilliant light.

Every passing night she sees the creatures of the day rest, peacefully enjoying their dreams as they swim in their sheets, and the creatures of night prowl looking for their meals. She fades from sight, losing a piece of herself every day. She hopes her precious treasures below are not frightened. She wishes not to leave them but every month it is the same, it is her nature.

Then when she returns, she is only welcomed by few. The ones who do recognize her loving light come out to witness her beauty every time she comes back to the world. She loves them the most, the ones that notice her return. They are the ones who dance in her beams, who smile as she smiles with a Cheshire grin, and who wish her a goodnight before they rest.

She loves these creatures so distant, so far from her. Never shall she fail with her love for them. They are companions, all in the galaxy that is so wide and strange. They change and develop, though their core features stay the same. She watches them watching her and she is happy.

Donnagan

This, insanely enough, was a dream of mine that I had at the beginning of 2019. It was as vivid as I tried to describe it here. I love legends about magical creatures and this story ties into the Medieval and Renaissance romantic tales. This might turn into a longer work later on but for now I wanted to let Donnagan be independent. Also, for non-Gaelic speakers here is the best translation I found "Tàimid caillte" means "We are lost." ~ K.E.

The negotiations were almost done. The Human King, as mighty as he was with his impatient advisors at his side, waited for that inevitable attack. The Faye King and Queen would not back down, each seated on their own black draft horses, watched the other ruler knowing this was not a battle they could win but they sat proud and tall. They had been hunted down and the army that now stood to face the humans was all they had left, not more than two hundred soldiers. The humans had six hundred displayed in front of them and this was just the main army. King Rowlan knew his troops outnumbered the Faye, but he didn't want the bloodshed to start.

He looked past the metal helm that sur-rounded his head and at the Faye. Proud people all and if there had been any other way to settle the dispute he would have done so. The negoti-ations that had been halted on this new battle-field were stopped because of his own advisors. They would not give the Faye any of their land. To them these proud people were nothing but murderous monsters that needed to be wiped from the earth. Across from King Rowlan was the Fayes' last general who was now the speaker for his majesties.

Donnagan was a dark Faye. His hair was pitch black; his skin was white as snow. His predatory eyes as blue and clear as sapphires. He saw everything. He was said to see into the hearts of men and determine their fate. But he never did. That is what King Rowlan liked about the steadfast general. He had the pleasure of meeting Donnagan in the peace talks. He was a quiet man who had opinions but kept them to himself unless he was asked. Never once would he tell what a man's fate was, no matter how long you pestered him about it. He would always say "The future is never set and there is no use lingering on what may never come."

Staring at Donnagan now, the King felt sick. He knew Donnagan was a warrior who had taken down many of the first humans who had gone hunting for the Faye, however, he could only think about the swarm of soldiers that would slice through the reserved warrior. The King of the Faye, who he never got a name from spoke loudly and clear over the battlefield.

"We want nothing but peace, yet we continue to be attacked. Even through these negotiations, my people are slaughtered. If there is to be no peace we will fight here and now to defend ourselves, our families, and our lands."

"Your lands?! You have none you animals! You steal, murder, and take what belongs to us and us alone!" Creev one of King Rowlans' twin advisors yelled back which irritated Rowlan.

"It is not your space to speak Creev" Rowlan snapped in a hushed tone. Creev was only fifteen if that; he was naïve and full of himself. Rowlan hated that about his advisors. All young, two which were twin brothers who had the exact same opinion about everything.

Rowlan turned his attention back to the King and Queen of the Faye "I will not fight with you today or any other day. Human and Faye are meant to live together not hunt each other. So, has it been, so will it always be." Creev turned to him with an abhorred look but King Rowlan took no notice. He turned his stead around. His Knights did the same following loyally. Rowlan did not realize Creev refused to listen to such words.

Creev, once outside of the sight of the King, motioned his men forward and started an attack of his own. Donnagan watched as the human Creev ran forward with blood thirst in his eyes. He readied himself as the blonde bowl-cut hair bounced on the brow of a young and spiteful child-man whose voice raised in a scream of rage. Creevs' sword raised high as he ran the short distance over the field towards the King and Queen of the Faye who had already turned to leave with their army shortly in pursuit. But now the peace was broken, the humans lead by Creev, were attacking and there was no way the Faye were going to stop them.

He yelled at the King and Queen who were surprised their horses rearing and pawing anxious of the approaching men. "Ride! We will stop them! Leave!" he faced this menace as he always had and ran forward at Creev who was solely focused on the King and Queen. A few of the frontline Faye ran forward with him to meet the humans so that the others could escape. Creev didn't see him. Donnagan was astounded as he came up on the boy and stabbed him through the stomach. Creev never saw him his rage did not show him his enemy and for that Creev was shoved off Donnagans sword and lay sprawled on the ground gasping as he died. This was no longer Donnagans focus as he rushed forward into the horde of humans that kept coming in Creevs' wake.

Donnagan could see Creevs' brother on the side lines waiting to come forward into the fray but the human King was on his way back. He must have heard the battle through the forest he had entered and rounded back to stop the fighting. Donnagan was now swarmed with human soldiers, fifteen at least, but he was parring and slashing with little hope that the humans would stop. He could feel the slices and punctures trailing over his body as he could not keep up with so many weapons. His mind swam as pain started to envelop him, but he kept swinging.

King Rowlan saw the mighty Donnagan surrounded and bleeding. Faye blood was a silver white and there was plenty pouring out everywhere. He cantered over as quick as his horse would take him until finally in front of him, not thirty yards away a spear pierced through the Faye General's chest making him quake and stop. The spear was removed but Donnagan tried to stay standing his eyes glazed over as if dreaming.

He fell to the ground breathing harshly. King Rowlan yelled over the commotion just as the spear was raised once more to silence the General for good "Get back! Do not dare raise your weapons to him! You fools!" The men backed away hearing the order. They should have stayed away from the fight to begin with. King Rowlan dismounted quickly, his knights following suit. Gently he rolled Donnagan over, so his face was to the sky. Blood ran like a flood out of his mouth and he stuttered murmuring Tara.

Rowlan knew of Tara, the White Faye who lived in a hidden garden in Nel Nor Woods. It was rumored some time ago that Donnagan had begun to court her. Now that would never be. Donnagan's blood pooled around him touching the Kings cloak and boots. "Oh, friend this should have never happened to you."

He coughed and wheezed his last words, staring into Rowlan's eyes "Dear King bring me to Tara take me to her. I have been nothing but loyal. Bring me to my Taar..." His voice chocked on the overwhelming amount of blood that poured out of his mouth. His eyes closed slowly without focus. He was gone and King Rowlan knew what he had to do.

"I want no one to disturb him. Fetch a wagon and water. His body shall be cleaned and redressed in the finest clothes. Mend his armor as well. We will take him back to his lover for proper burial." The Knights nodded separating out into two groups, one to guard the body the second to stop the soldiers from attacking any more Faye. Some ushered the killers away to do the bidding of the King. "This is a sad day friends, when one so loyal to his people, is killed by treachery. It will be hard to renue the friendship that this meeting was supposed to acomplish." King Rowlan left on his horse to follow the Faye to try and rekindle the shattered friendship.

Crise saw an opportunity to avenge his

brother's death as he saw the King leave. He walked up to the four Knights that waited for the wagon to take the body. They snarled and huffed at his approach which he sneered in aggravation.

"What do you want Crise?"

"How dare you speak to me like that I'm the Kings Advisor! I am more important than you, so respect me! Now let me through I want to see how much work we will have to do to repair his body." The men narrowed their eyes at him then returned to looking out for the men who stumbled back from the battlefield cussing at the Faye. One closest to Crise mumbled "Rat" under his breath as the advisor walked past into their makeshift circle.

Once they were decently distracted, he smiled and kneeled next to Donnagans head. He quietly unsheathed his hunting knife gently pressing it into the Faye generals throat and quickly sliced through till it was cleanly separated. Behind him the guards were screaming at a group of his brothers' men. He severed the spine with a sickening crunch. Off the proud Faye's head came.

He smiled standing up with the head and ran to his horse. The Knights screamed and chased after him. He outran them and was able to gallop away back to the camp. He raised the head high for all the troops to see.

"Donnagan the mighty Faye general is

Dead! Treason for killing my brother! This vermon is dead! We killed this high and mighty Faye! They will run from our power! No more shall we fear the Faye!" The men hollered in delight. Crise smirked. The King would never win this peace treaty.

* * *

Tara gasped as she felt her lover lose his essence. She fell to her knees only few minutes before as she had felt Donnagan die. But now, now his pride, his dignity, his essence, his soul was gone. He would be trapped wandering in the place of the lost and dishonored forever without her. She crawled to the edge of the gardens pool.

Her tears fell into the water creating soft ripples. She whispered softly to the pond. "Show him to me". The water swirled and clouded finally revealing a moving image of the child named Crise, holding Donnagans head up by the hair, revealing it to the human encampment. The show was met by loud cheers before the young welp stuck her loving Donnagans head on a stake parading it around. She cried out in rage and pain before yelling out to the forest "Tàimid caillte".

Bound Marriage

I started this as a small vocabulary paragraph which has grown and developed, but I have always imagined it as being a short story. Like many of the stories in this collection Bound Marriage was never meant to be more than just a glimpse into a different world. Much like a dream. ~ K.E.

The aroma of the roses floated down the aisle as the gracious and elegant bride walked. Her groom was a haughty man with no respect for her life. He was a Baron, wealthy enough to be near to the King and an advisor occasionally. She was a beautiful maiden from a dying line of Knights with no favor of the King.

"The frequency of a marriage at the capital is rare but because our bride is a Nymph we will except." She remembered as she walked down the aisle. The King smiled as he did before when he had looked upon her and accepted the marriage request between her and the Baron. Her breath came quick and quiet as she prayed that the Demon King would end the war after their wedding. He had promised her if she married this Baron, it would reclaim her families social standing and then everything would end. Her people would be left to have good lives instead of death and tragedy.

'The weight of the realm is on me' she thought as she walked up the stairs to meet her new horrible life. She would be left alone mostly while her new husband traveled through the Dimensions hopefully creating peace. She desperately wanted ceasefire but knew that the many different worlds were nothing but a monopoly to this despicable King. Her original lover, a young dishonored Knight, had left her to help the resistance. Now she was left wondering if he was dead and if she was making the right choice.

Oh, how she wished her fate would have found her a true prince. A man that would have fought off the Demon King and restored peace to the lands. She wished that a strikingly handsome man would burst through the castle doors and save her from the chaos she had chosen to accept for the betterment of her people. This was for them, not for her and she would never forget that. But she could still dream or so she thought. The hand maid gently fixed her train just as she had reached the steps in front of the throne. The music quieted, she faced the baron, her soon to be husband. She stared at the face of a killer but refused to cry out of spite. She took one last glance at the door. As it slowly shut her hopes disappeared with the fading light.

Broken Crown

This is based off of one of my dreams about the idea of the fairy folk. Broken Crown captured my heart in a wrenching way. Somehow with many of my characters I tend to fall for the ones with strong ties to family and their children. This story inspired so much creativity in me that I can't let this imagery die. ~ K. E.

The night was dark, but a gentle warm breeze swept over the land. The summer night caressed the Kingdom and encouraged the calm of the mythical creatures that inhabited the land. The Princess, however, was not asleep. In her own room she screamed out in agony her lips curled and her fangs biting into towels to muffle the sound. Her legs were propped up and she was pushing as hard as she could. The labor was stalled, and she could do nothing but push. The Prince was asleep in his own bed halfway across the castle near his parent's room.

He had refused to bed her after the incident. He had refused to look at her. He wanted nothing more than a male heir, but he didn't want one right now not with his succession of his father only weeks away. So, he slept peacefully with no disturbances while his wife groaned in agony.

The pain and pushing lasted all night till finally the child was born just as the sun peaked over the mountains. The Princess wept happy for the child but also because the pain ceased. Her face was a sickly green and covered in sweat. She smiled and laughed in relief just as the nurse, an older Faye woman with delicate wings, handed her the bright red-haired child that whimpered softly. The Princess took her new baby girl softly hugging it to her and began to coo a soft old hymn to calm her. The child was healthy. Her red hair was soft red fuzz on her head. The Princesses smile lingered on the child as she rocked it back and forth. She was in love for the second time in her life. This child was hers.

The nurse leaned over whispered in a concerned tone "She looks nothing like you or the prince my lady. He will be upset."

The Princess still with her humming voice said "She is heaven sent that is why she is different my husband will understand. I have been faithful to him all my life. He will understand. We will tell him in the morning for now let him rest. He will soon see his daughter and love her."

But when he arose in the morning, he did quite the opposite. When he saw the child as the Princess came to present herself to the King, Queen, and Prince, he was outraged. The rulers were all outraged. She was not one of them this creature though born a vampire was not his and he refused to believe otherwise. The King sneered looking over at his wife "What a disgrace this woman is! She dares to bring such filth into this home claiming that is our granddaughter?!"

"She is not our daughter in-law! I refuse to claim that child as my granddaughter! Look at her she looks nothing like any of us!" the Queen stuck her nose in the air as the Prince yelled loud enough that his voice echoed in the room and woke the child, which cried softly into her mother.

"How dare you, tramp! This is not my child! Look at her red hair! We both have black! This is an impossibility unless you really did sleep with that wolf so long ago! That knight whom expressed such interest in you! You deserve death for this you scarlet!"

"I have done no such thing! This is your child, that you bore ten months ago! Her vampire blood is pure and untarnished! She has been sent to us by the heavens to bring a new light into this world!"

"A new world?! You expect that rat to be my heir?! I will never accept this creature as my heir or even my daughter!" he raised his hand and came down hard on his wife's' cheek. She clutched the child tight to her chest as her face whipped to the side. She only said two words.

"Yes Sire."

She bowed her head gently attempting to

make a curtsy though she was unused to the child in her arms, before leaving the throne room of the hateful family she had married into. Once the doors were behind her, she ran with her child to her room and packed as much of the infant clothes she could into a small satchel, leaving the baby in the cradle nearly asleep.

The Princess sang through her tears lulling her daughter into a soundless sleep. When the Princess got to her own dresser the royal crown lay gently on the ornate pillow awaiting the day her husband would become King. She knew what she would do. She gently tucked the crown of pearls, diamonds, emeralds, rubies, gold, and silver into a small pouch wrapped gently with red fur and linen. Then she waited patiently.

For hours the Princess and her child waited for the light to fade. She waited anxiously pacing the room till finally the moonless sky descended the land into darkness. As soon as it did, she bolted for her chance at a better life. She ran through the secret passages of the castle all the way down to the stables with her little girl and the two bags. A horse was already waiting for her saddled and bridled. The Princess looked around and saw no one. A note lay gently on the saddle.

My Princess,
I know that you could not choose me but because of my love for you I will save you and your daughter. She is not mine, but I will protect her. Go to the little village in the woods to the north where my grandmother lives. There I will meet you within a few months' time. Safe travels my Princess.

She stuck the note into the bag shaking her head. "If only I had met you first my wolf. This child would have been yours." Mounting the horse as quickly and gently as she could she took her child and fled to the small village. It was days away, but she never stopped for rest. She fed her daughter as they went. Her steed held up well as he was as determined as his mistress. She arrived at night, the village mostly quite had only a few lights on in the cottages and what looked like the tavern.

She looked about unsure where the house was when a small frail old woman with silver hair came hobbling out on her cane. "This way dear. I will keep you safe." The old woman gently took the reins and lead them to the far side of town where a small cottage just the woman's size lay tucked away.

"How did you know I as coming, my husband condemned me just a few days ago."

"My dear grandson feared for you and your unborn child and told me months ago to be ready to receive you. So, when he told me days before you were due that I must be prepared I began to walk out to the edge of town each night to collect some roots for some medicines. I'm glad and horribly sorry that tonight you should find me."

The Princess looked down at her child who gently started to stir, her eyes opening to catch the star light. "I am most sorry as well. I wish it could have been different."

"Will you go back to your husband's wrath?"

"To protect her, yes.... I will tell him that she fell ill and that I left to morn my child alone. He will be glad to get rid of her..." Her voice trailed off just as the baby reached up for her mother. The Princess smiled then leaned down to kiss her forehead. "I hate to leave her...and the prospect of having a life with your grandson... But I made a promise till death do we part. And this will be the only way to keep her safe from my husband."

The grandmother nodded softly leading them to the front where she tied up the reigns to the fence of her small garden. The rest of the night the Princess stayed making sure her little joy would have everything she needed to grow healthy and strong. Before she left in the morning, she handed the old woman a note for her werewolf Knight and the boxed crown saying "Tell him I do love him and someday maybe we could be together. This box is for her when she is old enough and after my husband is gone from this world. Give this to her and tell her... tell her, her mother would love to have her home. I will outlive him for her." With these final words she left her darling child to the protection of the werewolves. The royal crown stayed hidden in the small box underneath the old wolfs bed until the soon to be King had passed. It waited for the one whom it belonged to blossom into an adult.

War-Boy

A small tale about a simple and humble beginning, this narrative is very modest. I wanted to capture a part of a life long forgotten but also make it a bit fantastical. It was never meant to be more than a glimpse into the life of a small seemingly useless child, but I believe it brings more to the table than it first appears. ~ K.E.

The slave folded the stiches into the clothes. His master was in the war for freedom. He dismantled every inch of the little pieces of armor that was bestowed upon his master. "The earth will populate no demon.". he said to himself. He remembered the Knight's words and nodded. There would never be a demon left if only he was strong enough. He would save his village eventually. He would become a Knight in no time. He had practiced the swordplay that the soldiers and Knights had learned. He went through the motions every single night before bed and again when he awoke the next morning.

"But I could be on the battlefield, I could win this war. I am left out of these battles." He looked away remembering what he promised to his mother. He planned a speech to his father and mother before he took up the Knights offer of becoming a squire. He had hardly known that had meant he would be a glorified slave when he first started. His father was embarrassed at what he heard. "Your frame is too small, and you do not have a dignified personality. You will no more be a Knight then I will be a nobleman. Give up your dream boy, you're a farmer." He looked away and dismissed the thought.

The boy took the laundry to soak it in the soupy waters he had prepared earlier. He remembered his mother telling him that he would be a good knight. Even now so far from home he could remember her tender quiet nature. She was not a woman of many words, but you could feel her emotions rather than hear them. When she said something, it wasn't the words, it was the heart behind it. The memory of her smiling made him smile as well. "I'll become a knight for the both of us mama."

He fixed the Knights armor, washed his clothes, before running off to the cook's tent for some food. He was going to train harder tonight than he ever had before, then maybe just maybe he would save the Knights life, fighting the demons off tomorrow when the battle arrived.

For the last hour of the day, just before dusk he went behind the Knight's tent and trained until he fell asleep at its base. He dreamed that he slaughtered all the demons and saved the Knights from their ultimate doom. His small body was clothed in the finest armor that he had ever seen. Once he had protected the Knights, he pushed forward destroying the demon horde until he reached the King of all the demons. Mighty and gruesome with a head of a bull, antlers the size of forty men, the Demon King wore armor made up of human skulls. With one fell swoop the little war boy took the mighty beasts head off. He stood on top of the body as all the Knights surrounded him crowning him King.

"Boy! Boy! Where are you?! Hurry Boy the battle is about to start!" he woke up at the base of the tent right where he had fallen asleep. Startled at the yelling he rushed into the tent and saw his master slowly and clumsily trying to dress himself. "There you are! Quickly now I need to get ready! They have advanced their march on us.!" The little boy ran over quickly to get his master dressed and before he knew it the Knight was charging out of the tent to battle. He was left alone once more. He would not be going to battle today.

Goddess

Upon having another one of my expansively dramatic dreams, this became one of the 2019 stories that I couldn't quite understand what I was writing until it was completed. This story was somewhat inspired by the true Greek mythologies and those of the Percy Jackson series by Rick Riordan. ~ K.E.

The gods all had a guard, demi humans, to be exact. They would change us out every two hundred years or so since demi humans don't live forever. We the God Guards were to protect and obey the wishes of our god, mine was Persephone. She unlike the other gods was a bit harder to protect as she had to travel from Earth to the Underworld about every six months and many of the vengeful gods would try to kidnap her. She often told me that I was her favorite guardian. She was sincere, however, I'm positive she has said that to every guardian she had.

Today had been a day I did not want to be a guardian. Hades, god of the Underworld, yelled at my goddess shaking all of the realm. It was two days before she had to leave to go back to the surface to see her mother.

"You must obey me! You don't understand I must have the joy of destroying the others and for this I must have your guard!"

"How dare you! Obey You?! No! She is mine why don't you use your own?!" Hades let out a grunt as he was scolded.

"I cannot he is too weak and I have sent him out on another mission."

"Have you forgotten the last time I left her with you?" her arms crossed "She was covered in burns from the fires of Hephaestus and I had to spend three of my months on earth nursing her back to health. Besides that, what on earth do you want her for?! You have an entire undead army at your fingertips."

At this Hades snapped his fingertips and a new bone door appeared next to him. "Follow me my Queen and I will show you my plans." He pushed open the door and let her into a massive room. It was large enough for the gods and I was only half her size, standing only up to her waist. Hades motioned us forward and I followed my goddess in.

"Here is my ultimate plan of attack my dear, all gods will have to obey me with this at my fingertips." He motioned to the center of the black carved stone room where a large bronze and gold contraption sat. Massive disks that were as tall as I was and as thick as I was tall , were aimed at the door. The contraption was covered in ancient spells that were written by the Titans themselves. The contraption had inner circles laced together with intricate patterns that connected each other.

I stared at it looking confused as I tried to decipher the strange spells, but Hades spoke up excitedly, happier than he had ever been before.

"It is my . . . our way of getting out of here my darling. This device can ensnare the other gods and give their power to me. I can become King of Olympus; I have even sent out a messenger to fetch Hermes and Artemis to be my test subjects. Shall we try?"

Persephone looked at the machine with an awe-struck face. I looked back and forth between the two. He was serious, but he was not threatening my goddess. She just looked down to me as Hades smiled and caressed his newfound weapon.

"Do as he says Lenoa, I trust you to take care of this." She leaned down and whispered "We lead my husband to his doom; I will use it against him." She stood back up and hugged her husband gently "That sounds amazing my dear when shall they be here?"

From behind us a small twinkling sound came from the foyer of the palace. Persephone had installed that the first moment she was able to change things. Hermes and Artemis were shown into the chamber by Charon, who normally did not leave his ferry except for the gods. He left immediately after. Both gods were followed by their guards. I circled them softly making it look like I was heading out the door. Whatever my goddess desired she would have. They watched me all the while.

Hermes spoke first very concerned "I was told to come see you immediately. Is something wrong? Are souls not coming down here?" He was a bit skittish when it came to the underworld.

Hades shook his head "No, nothing like that."

"Then why am I here? I thought I would need to hunt souls down and retrieve them." Artemis narrowed her eyes and put her hands on her hips.

"No, no, nothing like that."

Hermes started to get upset "Then what is it Hades? Do you realize I have a lot on my plate at the moment?"

Hades nodded at me and motioned me to close the door. "I wanted to show you something very valuable" I closed the doors gently, no mortal could have moved them. "See this machine is wonderful" He flipped the switch on, and it started to rev up and glow, aimed right at Artemis and Hermes. They looked panicked. "This however can steal your essence" at which point he snapped his fingers; I immediately attacked the other guards. They knew of me but they had never fought me before nor had they seen much of my combat.

We danced around slicing and hacking at each other. I kept them at bay until Hades had powered up the machine.

"What is that?! What are you doing?!" Hermes tried to fly towards the machine, but it was already powered. They had been sufficiently distracted and Hermes got the full brunt of the bright white light that shot out from the machine. Before the guards could react to Hermes being shot, I sliced through the throat of Artemis' guard with my gladius. I sliced through the back of Hermes' guard and severed his spine as Artemis was shot with the beam. The guards crumbled down just as I looked up to see the gods fade into white brightness and ash.

Hades laughed maniacally and smiled at Persephone. "See my love?" Hades flipped a switch and turned the machine back on. The power came out on the other side where Hades stood standing and it started to make him glow ith the combined force of the other two gods. Once it finished, he switched it off and came back around to show off his newfound aura and looked at the ash piles that lay in front of me. He smiled with glee. "Look what I have become! I can accomplish everything now! I can take back Olympus for my own!"

Persephone rounded the machine and went to the switches. "Yes, my dear husband you could accomplish anything but I ... I could accomplish much, much, more." She flipped the switch immediately laughing.

"WHAT?!" Hades looked panicked and started towards the machine, but it was too late it glowed with the white light and seared into the god of the underworld tearing into his essence and destroying him. Persephone laughed evilly as all of his power drained. He screamed in agony. Then another pile of white ash lay before me. I looked to my goddess who was more than pleased with herself.

"I've finally done it my dear guard. He's finally gone, and I can do what I please."

"Yes, my goddess" I came up to the side of the machine and kneeled before her closing my eyes. I heard the machine flick on once more and this time it was aimed at her. The raw essence and magic that filled the room poured into Persephone. When I opened my eyes, the room had changed from its pitch-black stone to a hidden forest room. A large massive oak now covered the top of the mechanism, its roots gently reaching down on either side and into the floor. The bodies had fed the garden and grass grew all around. Her eyes smiled. She came over to me and kneeled.

"My dear guard you have done an excellent service for me. As a reward you shall forever guard this machine and this room. I will bring the other gods back to this very room and we shall ensnare them all. I will become goddess of all, and you will help me." She gently caressed my face and she looked as mad as Hades had been. Suddenly I felt very afraid. I would be trapped with her forever and there was nothing I could do.

"Yes, my goddess." She smiled with cheer

and stood up to leave.

Outsider

I have never been able to stray away from the idea of an outsider who sees it all. It shapes many stories and characters; this happens to be one of them. It is another short tale, but I couldn't add more to it just like some of the others. It might later add to another story or possibly a longer book, but for now it remains this short story. ~ K.E.

I walked by the newspaper stand. The front page had a foreword about my race. The vampire and humans didn't really like us, the Wolfite. Well to be clear we were the ambition of the vampires' blood lust because of its sweet taste. It was much more natural than the tame humans. Every day there was an obituary of our deaths. If we were caught, they'd put a price on us. We seemed to the world to be nothing more than beasts ready for the slaughter though the humans or most of them did not devour us.

We were condemned in public and often led to slaughterhouses or farms. It was hard for us to hide what we were and what our natures were because our ears and tails always showed.

The leaders suggested purging solutions multiple times, but they would also say "You could never mistake a wolfite for a human or vampire." Which if we wore the dirty colored short clothes that we were supposed to no one could mistake us. Most of us were smarter than that we went into hiding.

It is getting harder to hide from the hunger driven vampires though. There is no way to truly escape the bloodbath. This was our life, and it would get worse unless we decided to fight back.

The Little Bear

*I smile every time I read this story because it reminds me
of my own childhood. My father loved to tell me stories
about Smokey the Bear and that was the biggest influence
for this story. Forest fires had a huge impact on my child-
hood because of my father's job as a firefighter and my
love for cute animals, thus this story. ~ K.E.*

I stood there and watched her and how she
moved. Digging didn't look that hard. I decided I
would go help her. They say don't go around the
back of any working project and I didn't listen
to that rule. For that I was rewarded with a big
pile of dirt in my face. I don't blame mom, she
didn't know I was there. Soon enough she did find
the honeycomb she was looking for and was very
pleased. I went down in the hole and dug to get a
piece of my own. By the time I got mine, mom was
almost done. She started giving my muzzle a clean-
ing and I cleaned hers. Honey can be very sticky.

Soon mom went back to work, and I was
busy swatting those darn bees. Then I heard a rock
fall from behind the tree. The cliff wall had many

rocks stuck to it, but this was just a little one. Mom looked up once and paid no mind to it again. It happened again but this time big rocks fell. I hid behind mom and noticed one fell on her. Once the rocks stopped, I tried to dig her out, I cried to her to wake up, but she was sleeping too well. I cuddled up next to her and cried to see if that would wake her up. I soon fell asleep myself.

I woke up to a whispering voice. "Run down the hill. Run down the hill." I looked up to see a little butterfly. "Run downhill." Oh, if I went down the hill, I was sure mom, who was still sleeping, would wake up and come looking for me. I trotted my proud self-down the side of the hill tripping a few times. Soon I came upon a little frog. He hopped then I hopped. We did this repeatedly until he jumped into a stream. I liked that game and wanted him to come back, so I jumped into the water as well. It was so cold I jumped back out.

I looked at the water one more time. That frog was mean; he played with me then played a dirty trick like that? I cried for a second then curled up on the ground a little ways away. I slowly fell asleep and had horrible nightmares about the frog. Soon I groggily awoke to the smell of smoke. I wonder what it could be that was burning. I couldn't hear or see mom but there was a strange noise like a roar.

The fire became a monster and I could see it coming for me it wanted to eat me. I ran, ran far away from it looking back to make sure it wasn't catching me. Then something crinkly grabbed me up off the ground grumbling something through its horrifying monster face.

"Don't worry little cub I got you I won't let the fire eat you." I didn't understand what the creature said but he took me away, far away from the monstrous fire.

Fires Victory

This story came to be because of two seemingly broken hearts that I happened to get around the same time that this story was written. I was in my teen years so easily wavered when it came to my heartbreaks. This was the biproduct a way of empowering myself and a way of condemning the people who had broken my heart. I look back at it now and laugh a bit because this story is so directed by my old emotions and now . . . I've changed. ~K.E.

Fire is dangerous but a beautiful thing. You must stoke its flames very carefully. When this started, I was young. I was an nieve girl who was too blind to see the true intentions of other people. I suppose I got myself into that mess but then again everyone knows not to mess with fire.

I glared at the window. His eyes were promulgating his apologies. His face was dark and tired. The man those eyes belonged to was a beguiling creature with a darker side that everyone feared. For a second, I believed he was truly sorry. My heart ached for the affection that came with his desires, but my mind knew all too well how many pieces the poor organ had been shattered into already. My heart now too unrepairable would not be broken again. The fortitude of the metal door separating us was amazing. He was known to destroy what he did not want. Many would consider me lucky to escape. It wasn't luck; it was the bolstering of my will.

His smile faded as mine grew wide as a Cheshire cats and he realized he had lost. He began to kick and punch at the door like a wild animal.

"Ha, you stupid man, you should never have messed with fire." I was overwhelmed with joy, but I could not help it. I turned my back towards him and walked out of the confined hallway that led to the door. He screamed so loud that it should have woken the dead. I put my generals cap on and walked out into the prison's main halls. Every officer saluted me with smiles that mimicked my own. I garnered my lieutenants and left the huge despairing building with nothing less than a victory in my mind.

My great black and white shire strode in front of the other officer's steeds. At first, I had little to say. My officers asked happily about that man's capture and why I hunted him down with such a ferocity, but I did not answer. My smile just grew wider. After escaping the sight of the building, I could no longer keep my happiness bottled up.

"Hiya!" My gelding leaped into a gallop with an alacrity that was refreshing to my mood. I raced on the road back to my manor house. My officers in quick pursuit behind me were trying their best to keep up. They soon realized this is what I wanted, joy and fun. Soon they played along. I laughed at the top of my lungs with the luxury of freedom. We rode to the front of my manor and jumped off our panting horses. My officers and I stumbled through the front door laughing with such joy my maids looked concerned.

"Prepare dinner and let us drink my best ale!" I hollered to any attendant that would listen.

During dinner the men tried to conjure up more information about the criminal they saw locked behind that metal door. I gave them only simple facts about how I caught him. Cornered him I should say. I told them no matter how much I hated the devil, I could not kill him due to my chaste mindset. My head started to buzz with the bitter sweetness of the ale and my propriety started to slip away. They soon ushered me into the parlor and gave me water to sip. My mood soon changed sitting with all the lights out except for the burning fireplace. The darkness had set over the night. All the men quitted. "General?" one of my officers quietly questioned interrupting the silence.

"You have pestered me more than twain of the story about that man. Though he is a murderer you are not satisfied to know that is the only reason why I hunted him." I slowly twirled the water glass in my hand. I looked at nothing but the red of the fire.

"General we all know that there is another reason why you hate that man." I heard the officer shift his weight awkwardly. He was nervous. If I was drunk, I might have become outraged and stripped him of his rank, right now I was just tired. He was young and knew nothing of holding his tongue.

"Yes, there is another reason why I hunted him. It is not just the hate of a charlatan that I hold against him. No, it is much fiercer than that. I hate him with a passion that holds my mind fast and my heart secure."

"Why didn't you just kill him then General? You had the most perfect opportunity when you cornered him at the end of the hunt." I smiled and relaxed back into my chair.

"I was once a young woman who trusted in everyone too much. My censure was clouded with thoughts of love. I suppose I gave it away in bounteous quantities. He was a man I gave my trust to. I met him in those days, and I could not have regretted it more until now. He was a charming devil to me. Until..." I shut my mouth. This was painful for me to remember. "It was jealousy that ruined my love for him. And I suppose now that it was for the better." I swallowed another swig of water. "I was fraught with love for him. At first, we were the loyalist of lovers. You could see us happily strolling down the streets. But there was something deadly wrong with it. When we were, alone, he abused me, and he would never listen to my pleas for him to stop. But I wanted his love so much to the point where I ignored all his brutal tactics. My pith was nothing compared to his major plans. Of course, my jealousy raged. He started to get less interested in me. He would constantly see other women." I felt my anger and rage spit up in flames within my soul.

"He gave me one bauble, but it was little to nothing when I heard where the wretch had gotten it." Small growls slipped out of my throat as I spoke. "He was such a wicked wretch and then he left me. I in turn spit fiery words at him. I spoke all words of hate in this language and that! Ha, and then he did nothing! All he said was that 'If I had shown that passion before he might have loved me!'" I slammed my fist down on the armchair making it creak in pain. Everyone within the room jumped. I took one more swig and again relaxed.

"You won't believe me when I tell you what happened next."

"What General? What happened?"

"I slowly but surely got over him. Faster than I had expected I would actually. But he did not. I could see his inner turmoil growing. He needed someone to direct what little emotion he had on to. And without me he was angered easily. He could see me with other men that I fancied, and he became a ticking clock waiting to run out of time. His inordinate behavior was unacceptable. That's when I joined the military. He kept a close watch on me though, even when I was assigned.

He followed me and chased off any man who took any interest in me. Ha! His jealousy led to his downfall. He went insane without one person to take his worst out on. And that's how he became a murderer."

"But General if you had gotten over him why would you hunt him down like you did?"

"I saw that he was a monster and I knew how he would act. It's shameful to take out your pain by killing others. It's not only shameful but it is wrong, and I would not let the monster he became kill innocents." I got up and walked to the window. The moon slowly crept out from behind the clouds. "He is a monster. But I know one thing that all monsters fear. They fear the fire."

Bond

*I created this on the old forgotten website called Quizilla.
I used to write many stories and take hundreds of quizzes
through the website and this is one of the various tales
that I started to write. Originally it was intended to be a
long-standing series but as the site was shut down so did
the idea. I however have again grown fond of it once more,
maybe something will come out of it. ~ K.E.*

(Kyoko's POV)

I ran as fast as I could. No one would catch me but I just couldn't stop the Takers from destroying those innocent lives I wasn't able to save. I turned back for an instant to see the smoke rising. There were no more screams, the Takers had killed everyone even my teammates. "I was supposed to protect all of them." my voice was hoarse.

Somebody grabbed me and pulled my body through the portal. "Let go!" I yelled. The face I expected was not who was there. "Ray I thought the Takers got you?"

"They did, but I escaped." he gave me his best smile.

My knees gave in at when I realized that

everything I worked for was completely destroyed. "Brother what did I do to wrong? I followed all the regulations for our mission."

He looked into my eyes "They were expecting us." the voice of my brother did not comfort me.

"How?!" I yelled "How could they have known? Ray you're my brother tell me how?!" My voice rang throughout the room and down the hall. X came running. Tears flowed down my face like they never had before.

"What happened?" X's voice was desperate. "Where is everyone else?"

Ray repeated what he had told me. There wasn't a smile on his face anymore. The portal rang its' mellow tune which meant someone was coming. I grabbed my pistol, Ray brought out his metal strings and X took out a tiny pistol with a lot of power. We waited for what came.

(Arein POV)

I checked the room making sure I could bring in my delivery safely. I slowly jumped out the window onto the tree where the Protector was. Her eyes were still shut thankfully. I could only imagine what would happen if the Death Keeper found out what I had done. Her body was cold almost lifeless as I lifted her up into my arms. I jumped back onto the windowsill knowing one false move could kill us both. My feet hit the floor with no sound as I came in from my mission. I laid the unconscious girl on my bed. The moon shone in from the window and hit her face perfectly.

"She's beautiful Arein where did you get her?" I jumped at the sound of K's voice.

"How did you get in here?!" I yelled so loud my lungs hurt and the girl began to stir.

"You left the door open. What is she? She's not human. Wait is that a… That's a Protector. Arein what are you doing with it in here! Matoa is going to have you beheaded!"

His fear was unnecessary. "K its all right he won't find out I've done this before." His eyes went wide with horror.

"WHAT?!" The pain I saw in him was unbearable. I turned to the window. He was trying to be strong, but I knew he was scared, not for himself but for me. I glanced over my shoulder to see him standing there, tears running down his face.

"K, you need to trust me I will be fine." He closed his eyes and clenched his fists, the tears streaming down his face. "Brother" I said softly trying to calm him.

"No. If you want to throw away your life go ahead."

My already torn, beaten, and bruised heart had a new crack. His shouting voice was a punch to the stomach and his tears were razors slicing my arms and legs. He ran out of the room slamming the door behind him. My eyes gazed at the door. I was shocked that he would care that much about something like this.

"Ugh!" I spun around to look at the girl but

instead got hit in the face with a pillow. "Shut up fluffy wolf I want to sleep. I'll play with you in the morning Okay. Just go to sleep!"

"I must've drained too much energy from you." I whispered to her knowing she didn't understand. I laid one of the extra blankets on the floor. My body lay still but my mind was every where at once.

(Summer POV)

"She's been gone too long it should have only taken a couple of minutes; I mean come on!" Ray complained. We had known each other since we were five, we were like sisters. I'm the childish fun loving one and she is my big sister hard minded. Even though we're about the same age that's how our relationship worked. Ray groaned again.

"Ray please stop. I'm worried too, but we need to stay calm." He waited and looked at me trying to read my expression.

"I'm sorry for making you worry even more. Are you okay?" His body moved towards me.

"I'm fine! I just need ... I need to get out!" I ran out of the room tears starting to fall and I kept thinking about why he had to work up my worries so much. Couldn't he just fake being hopeful? He was her brother. She was probably dead. This was our job. It was dangerous and we never came back and said 'Honey, I'm home'. I heard him following me, but I slammed my rooms door behind me.

Hoping that he would stay out, I went to the

window and cried hard. Probably harder than I've cried in a long time. I heard the door creak open. "Get out!" I yelled through my sobs. He walked up to me, his arms wrapping around my waist.

"I'm sorry." He whispered, flipped me around and laid his sweet lips on mine. His lips were smooth as they grazed over mine. I lowered my head pressing it against his chest. "She will come back I know she will." His voice was soft and reassuring. I hoped he was right.

The Girl and her demon

At this time, I had started to think about all of the types of supernatural creatures and how most are shown in different lights. Specifically, demons, they became a concept to me that was different than most mythologies had portrayed them. I started to think of them as a shapeshifting shadow-like race tormented with the deadly curse of their name. There is another race called demons that are the traditional concept of demons. That's how this story started to come into being. ~ K.E.

There once was a girl who lived in the world of magic and knew more than anyone else about the fairies who hid, the horses that fly with the wind, and the energy that flowed through the world. One day she found a young demon, he was 16, a year older than the girl.

"Hello. Is something wrong?" her voice melodious.

"Yes, my father is trying to destroy all things good." He growled. "Who are you?" The demand in his voice scared her.

"My name is Etiona. What is yours?" she stuttered.

The demon boy paused for a moment looking at the ground. Maybe she did not know what he was. He tried to make up a name for himself, but she stopped his thoughts.

"I'm sorry I forgot demons usually never have names. Did I offend you in anyway?" the politeness in her overcame his bad mood.

"No, you did not" His voice softened "But how do you know what I am?" Many questions ran through his head, but no answers were clear.

"I study magic from this special book." she pulled out a leather-bound journal wrapped in leather strips of reds, browns and black from her bag and handed it to him. He opened it to reveal countless handwritten and drawn pages that were about the entire magical world. "This book tells me most things, even a bit of history of the races and other such facts." Her energy seemed to flow through the air like a light breeze.

"This book is the rarest in all the worlds, created by a great sorcerer. How did you get it?" his shock came out so fast that he didn't know how to control it.

"Well, I found it in the forest when I was five and I've been studying it ever since. I'll show you some of the power I have learned from it and what I can control."

Etiona did as she said and conjured up a little bit of energy that floated into the air forming a ball in front of him. He tried to touch it, but it disappeared.

"You can do that?"

"Yes, and much more. I trained myself with one very powerful spell since I received the journal. It has allowed me to learn things quicker than an ordinary person would." Streaks of power ran through her and filled the surrounding air with a calm aura.

He knew then that this girl, being as powerful as she was, would become something that no one would be able to stop. She was magic. In any case because of her power, his father would come after her. He stuttered sure of his decision to protect her.

"Do you mind if I stay with you?"

Another Holocaust Story

When I wrote this in middle school, I wasn't really the best writer, but I still loved it and kept at it. We were studying Ann Frank at the time and I investigated the other people who suffered during the Holocaust. I found it interesting, though not very surprising, that another group that suffered along with the Jewish people were the Gypsies. Thus, I tried my hand at telling a story about them. ~ K.E.

I think most people have heard of Anne Frank, but they don't know me. My name is Night Star. My family has and always will be Gypsies'. We're pious to our God as our ancestors were. This is the story of my tarnished life. I was born on a road in Germany, in 1930, everything was perfect. I learned to dance and sing in 1932 though I admit I was a distractible, eccentric young girl. By then the animal's intolerance for me was quite clear.

When I was three, Hitler came to power. I didn't fully understand then, but he seemed to activate a colossal amount of terror. My mom and dad were so worried. Then one day when we were on a road the police stopped us.

"Where are you filthy Gypsies going?!" they

barked. My father took them to the side and talked with them. After a few minutes he called to me.

"Night bring the money." I did as I was told. I was quite mature for my age which was at this time, four. After that we went into hiding.

We hid in the basement of an old women's house. I found her a nick name very fast. "Namy" I would say. She was a charitable lady, sort of like a grandma to me. I had many petty complaints about her basement though, such as "It's boring down here" and "Why is it so cold?" but my family never stopped loving me.

It was an invariable life in hiding. Until Namy found a young boy in 1936. He was six just like I was. We played and laughed for the years that we were there. I learned to confide in him with all my secrets. In truth, I started to have a crush on the boy.

In 1940, we were found out and taken to a concentration camp in Poland. I don't know the name neither do I care to know it. My family, my love, and I were all separated. Every day as I worked, I saw people come and go. Some would die in the living areas, others in the places where we worked. But through all that I kept my strength not knowing about my best friend or my father.

About midsummer 1943, my mother died of an illness which I had never heard of. A few days later I snuck over to the men's side of the camp. I found my father and my dear one, at night so the darkness could hide us. I told my father what had happened. That night I planned to escape. Five months earlier I had stolen sixty Reichsmark from a guard. We would sneak out to the front gates and pay our way out. We agreed to wait one month before this plan would start.

Half a month later I got word from one of the guards that my father had died. They said it was depression, but I knew that they had something to do with it by the way they smiled about it. When the night came to escape, I met my love and we paid for our freedom. The guards didn't ask where the money came from, but they were happy to get it.

After our grand escape we fled to the Allies. We met a young American soldier nicknamed "Fledge". He said he would give us money to go to America. He also said that we could stay with his wife and children in Boston. We agreed and thanked him.

When we arrived in America, we were greeted by Lady Liberty. In all my life I had not cried, but then when that beautiful lady appeared, tears fell like a waterfall. After Ellis Island we went to Boston. Fledges' wife greeted us with tears in her eyes. We stayed with the family until the end of the war. When I heard about the "Diary of Anne Frank" I decided to tell my story and that's my life from World War 2.

Goodbye from an Ordinary Girl

This story started with a prompt from one of my college creative writing classes. We looked at a picture online and the one that I came across was a note sitting on a log. The image inspired me so much that it happened to lead to this very story. I wanted to start it with a normal undertone and lead it into the fantasy style I enjoy. A note left alone stirs up the most intriguing part of the imagination. ~ K.E.

I sit alone waiting for him in the middle of the dark forest. I thought he would have been here by now. The moon shone bright as it reached the middle of the sky. It shines down in white streaks illuminating the forest making every small pine needle, leaf, branch, and even the earth glowed bright with the mysticism I hold so dear. It was strange to find that an ordinary girl like me could fall for an extraordinary man like him.

Roland was a tall man a foot or so taller than me, his white medium length hair would fall into his eyes that would often beg me to believe he was right. He always wore elegant clothing; otherworldly you could say. His red eyes would gleam with the intentions of mischief and fun. His pale skin complemented that of my own as if we were one in the same. We were moon beams that danced together.

I had to leave before the sun rose. Whether he would come with me or not was a different story altogether. I clutched the small journal to my chest. It was my release; I could say everything I wanted to in it. I could draw anything I wanted to. Its paper was specifically crafted just for me. I wrote my deepest thoughts down within it. I looked around once more. "Maybe he got confused, he must be in the clearing." I started to walk in the direction of wildflower meadow.

***

"No no no no no! Let me go! I must go to her!" I screamed at my captors in disdain. Blood trickled down into my eyes making me shake my head. They just stared and laughed at my chained, bruised, and bloodied body. I hated them, everyone of the deplorable creatures that stood in my way.

"Sit quiet, filthy little rich boy. You'll soon meet your girl again, when we put her broken body at your feet!" The grotesque mercenary laughed throatily.

"Don't you dare touch Faye!" I screamed at him with all the rage of a lion. Though we had accepted this world of hate, violence, and chaos I couldn't help but to scream for her, for me for all of this torture to be over. I stopped, breathing heavily, furious that I needed more air, but the men's' walky-talkies gurgled to life.

"Captain! Captain! We're taking heavy fire! Their comin' for him! Their comin'!" the man screamed while rounds of gunfire echoed before the transmission stopped.

"Damn! Damn! Damn!" the captain yelled before a bullet was fired into his heart. The whole room lite up with bullets for a minute before everything went dark. A man walked forward.

"Needin' some help there, rich boy?" Gunner my friend looked at me, smoking a cigar, with an automatic assault rifle resting along his side.

"Gunner I have to get to her! She's in trouble!" I strained against my chains. He took a puff from his cigar and walked over.

"Take it easy Roland I'll get you out." He took his set of lock picks and freed me within a matter of seconds.

"I need to find her now."

"Yeah man, yeah I get it. We'll find her don't worry."

It didn't take us long to get to the clearing after we had checked the meeting spot. I ran forward as the sun started to rise over the mountain range. I looked around praying that Faye was here. The clearing was just how I remembered it. Red, yellow, and blue flowers glimmered in the rising light.

Gunner coughed deliberately "Roland she's not here we should be headin' out. It's not safe."

"No, she has to be here!" I ran around looking into the forest to see if she was out there somewhere.

"She's not. Faye's gone. We have to get you out of here." I knew he was right. I turned and slowly followed him ashamed of my hope.

As the men left, they failed to notice on the log near the center of the clearing, a small piece of paper folded neatly. A message written out of heartbreak "I doubt that you will even miss me. Good bye."

New-Town

This was another one of my various assignment stories and as I write more, I begin to realize that most of my short stories originated from my classes. When I have a prompt or inspiration, I go with it and many of my classes gave me the chance to do such things. This, though not very much of a story, hints at other realities and inspirations that I have collected over the years. ~ K.E.

The accommodations for me were unclear as I walked through the halls of the apartment complex. A man came out of room 326.

"Are you lost young lady?" his pleasantry was odd for the big city, but I went with it.

"Not to be rude but aren't you about my age sir?" A devious smile grew on his face.

"How should I know how old you are. You're not supposed to ask a woman's age, right?"

I was a bit remorseful, but he was being pushy. "Maybe that's true but I'm not going to tell you my age. I don't know you and you don't need to know that."

"Aren't you a feisty one. But I'm sorry miss no matter your age you must leave only renters are

78

allowed in. I will have to notify the police." I froze and remembered my job and what I was.

"No, I live here see!" I motioned to my suitcase which had everything I owned. I knew the flirtatious tactics he was using, but I didn't know why he was using it. I noticed he was staring, and I looked into his eyes. They were beautiful, a silvery blue with some sort of mist. I circumnavigated away from his gaze and started to blush a deep red. I finally found my papers and looked at them they were upside down.

"So, you are lost. Let me see those." I gave him the sheets which he then turned right side up. A haughty laugh came from his lips.

"What?!" I demanded; a bit too defensive.

"I can't believe it. You are standing right next to it." I turned bright red. 'No one told me we had roommates.' He seemed to know what I was thinking and gripped my shoulders and turned me to face the door opposite his.

"That's yours."

I thanked him and quickly went into my apartment. I let a sigh escape my lips. 'I'm such an idiot.' I told myself as I went to my bedroom. My bag flopped onto the bed as I let the clothes fall out of the suitcase. "So ends day one."

Headstrong

This was based on an old experience of mine and it is still crystal clear in my head. It impacted me in a way that I don't think I could ever understand or put into words. This story was the best way to explain to others and myself what had happened and how I felt. ~ K.E.

My body was hunched over ready to pounce at my target. My legs were ready for the unspoken challenge that awaited me. I was excited, giddy really, ready for the chase. The playground was alive with the other kids playing their separate games. I felt like the ruler sitting upon my throne ready for the challenge.

My best friend, the advisor, sat next to me watching the spectacle with a happy smile. Our blue uniforms were hot but comfortable. The private school had made our skirts out of softer fabric that was movable and perfect for what awaited me.

"You can't catch me! You're not fast at all! I could outrun you easily!" He said.

The tan skinned brown haired boy with

square glasses looked at me with a cheesy smile across his face. I would get him. I was young but fast, my small body could move like a torpedo. I could beat every boy in the school yard. They wouldn't admit it just like this boy was denying my strength and power. I ruled the playground not him, not ever.

"I could beat you easily." I smiled

"She's fast she could beat you with no problem." My best friend smiled happily.

I could feel my grin unnaturally expanding on my lips. 'Cheshire Cat' I thought.

"I'll run and you catch me!" He was obnoxious but I would prove him wrong.

"Okay" my voice was an eager purr. "I'll give you a ten second head start. I'll catch you".

He nodded his approval and the instant I said one, he was off. My grin never failed. I could feel the adrenaline shivering through my veins. I didn't know what the word adrenaline meant or what it was exactly, but I could feel it.

His body looked so close even though it ran further and further away. My muscles tensed my eyes watching him like the predator I knew deep down I was.

"Ten" I whispered to myself and I was off. I could feel my feet hit the ground with ease. My ankle popped as it always had at that type of pressure and movement then I was gone. I had eyes for nothing but my prey. The world flashed by me with a quickness and stream of light.

He dashed across the cement basketball court the volleyball net streaming across it with the wires holding it aloft in the middle surrounded by the warm air. He was heading for it his scrawny legs not taking him far enough away.

His hands grabbed the one line of the net that lay in front of him. He threw it up over his head and kept running.

'Sneaky' my mind purred 'but not enough to save you.' I streaked after him my arms reaching out for the rope. I clenched my fingers around the cording throwing it up like the boy had done.

Something went wrong. My fingers didn't let go; the rope caught on its own momentum. It came back over my head and swung slamming right back against my neck. It took me by surprise as my body was thrown back.

It was dark for a while; I could feel myself laying on something colder than the air around it, not by much though. It was dark so dark. Then I was in the air being moved. I couldn't see, everything felt like it was blurry.

When I did open my eyes nothing was clear, colors blurred together. It seemed like the light streamed through stained glass. I was being carried upright as if I was walking. I wasn't walking though. 'Strange I didn't feel anyone grab me. I felt arms around my waist and nothing else. I thought it was my sister. I thought she was crying. 'Why was she crying?' I didn't know.

Everyone seemed sad for some reason. The

feeling swirled around me as I was carried off the playground and up the small cement staircase through the metal door. I don't remember much of the office itself just the people gasping in shock and horror.

'What's wrong?' I couldn't understand what all the fuss was about. My mind was so clouded. People kept trying to talk to me.

"Where does it hurt?"

"Here I found it!"

"No that's not it."

"Tell us where it hurts."

Couldn't they understand I couldn't feel it? It didn't hurt there was no headache, no migraine, no anything. It was just blurry. I didn't even try to focus but my eyes absently stayed straight.

I could see the rows of the brown-red wood pews covered in blue rough fabric. I saw the piano just in front of those and the white wall behind that. It was bright and dark in here. The shadows confused me as they melded with the streams of light.

They kept trying to talk to me and after a while I spoke a few words. Not many words came out of my mouth though, I suppose you need to think of words to say first. Sometime while I was sitting there my best friend's mom came and put the bandage on the area where my head was actually cut open. But I didn't feel her touch. I didn't feel the gauze.

She kept trying to coo me into talking but I

couldn't. She would also talk to the staff members that were there. I suppose she was trying to get them to do something, but I didn't understand.

After what seemed like a long time my vision cleared, it wasn't all foggy. I noticed I was sitting there holding my head alone. The grownups were in the office talking. I looked around and saw the sound system and the thin stained-glass windows on the far wall.

As I looked my head became dizzy once more. I barely remember my mom coming up and taking me out to the car. She sat me down in the front seat and called the doctor. She asked me how I felt after a few minutes of driving.

I was stable then too. I could speak, though I don't remember my words or hers. I could see and there was a dizziness. It seems like it wasn't long at all before I got to the hospital. She took me through the emergency entrance. That is when I learned that some people go into professions just for the money, not to help people

The nurse came up to us and told my mom that she would have to got into the waiting room and wait her turn.

"I called Dr. Galen myself and she specifically told me to come to this entrance!" She was so angry with that nurse.

We were led to a room or enclosed curtain area I couldn't picture it. I was seeing everything in a blur once more. I don't even remember laying down on the bed in the room. I do remember the medical machines glowing as only they do.

The doctor came in. I knew her or at least of her. She came in talked to my mom and tried to talk to me.

"We're going to have to stich you up okay. I'm going to numb the area, so you don't feel it."

She couldn't find it at first my hair being as thick as it was. It really didn't surprise me. When she found it though she had to shave a portion of it away so she could get to the cut itself. She took a needle which I did not see and pushed the numbing agent into my scalp. It worked quickly for the pain.

The pain killer didn't work how I had expected it to. I could feel her gloves working around cleaning up the mess that I couldn't imagine because all I thought was there was a huge cut. When the doctor started to stich me up, I felt it, I heard it. The needle being threaded had a distinct sound, a lone sound. There was silence except for the thread lacing itself into the needle.

The cold silver of the tool slipped in between my flesh over and over again. The feeling was so cold, the feeling was so strange as my head was slowly laced back together. She was done quickly which was unexpected.

It was lonely after that; I don't remember anything about what happened afterwards. I might have been driven to get an x-ray. I might have gone to get chicken nuggets. It was so weird it was like I lost all of that night.

I wish I didn't remember some of the things that happened over the days and weeks that followed. The boys teased me as usual. The meaner of the bunch would laugh at my failure. The nicer ones of the group would know when to be quiet. `

The school kept the volleyball net up despite how dangerous it proved to be. I would go out of my way to avoid the court. Making sure to step gingerly over the small bit of concrete before running through the gopher hole filled patch rectangle of grass.

I hated the injury as long as it was there. I had no freedom for the first week or so because I had to wear a wraparound bandage. It looked cool like a fighter, up until I went to school and was laughed at for it.

Showers were difficult then too. No water. The cut couldn't get wet or have soap on it. That in turn made me unable to wash my own hair until it fully healed. I don't think anyone could understand how grimy that was.

To this day I look back at what happened and ask myself questions. I'm intrigued by my own actions. I suppose I will never know why exactly I wasn't scared that day. Were you scared you were going to die? Many would ask. Truth was, no I wasn't scared.

Anger and sadness

This was created not to long before I began publishing this book. I wanted to show the depths of an emotion in a physical form. The prompt was to personify an emotion but of course I could not do just one emotion. Often when I deal with anger, sadness goes right along with it. ~ K.E.

I stared at the wall; Anger stared back. Its red and black fur sat tussled upon its haunches. Its smile was jagged sharp like a hyena or a jackal. I could see the scars over its eyes which made it blind. Its nostrils flared in heady anticipation. It knew what was coming. I didn't

"What's wrong?" my voice was a squeak so quiet. It just growled, extended its claws, and retracted them. Then within a few seconds it was everywhere in every corner of the room filling it with itself. It tore and gnashed and yowled. Pillows were flying being torn open. The books crashed and fell off the shelves, pages were ripped out. The laptop which I threatened to throw out the window so many times before, broke the glass and landed on the lawn shattering into a thousand pieces.

The lamps fell and the bulbs shattered upon the floor. The desk flipped over spreading all its contents, pencils snapped at the impact. Pictures fell and destroyed themselves. It clawed at the door and threw all the clothes out into the room ripping the shelves down out the closet. I shivered and watched as the chaos ensued.

It then turned its attention to me ripping open my skin, tearing out my heart, blinding my eyes, making me claw the bed. It felt like hours as the torture raged in our skins. After a while we both stopped and breathed heavily. Tears rolled down our faces. We yowled and howled and hollered loudly shaking the room. We quieted slowly.

Anger snarled and padded around me then left through the open window. Soft Sadness who was hiding under the bed crawled out, then climbed up behind me. It curled around me in a circle its big fluffy tail smothering me. The tears turned sad. There was nothing more I could do but sit here with Sadness and cry.

17925

Another one of the various stories I wrote for college, 17925 was a part of my idea that big brother is always watching. The rebellious teenager idea has always been an inspiration to me. This story was also just a part of my weird, fantastical dreams though it went into a different direction than I originally that it would go to. ~ K.E.

This school was trash. Only recently had she noticed how trashy it really was. It was by no fault of her own of course that she hadn't realized the grimy laminate tiles or the flickering yellow neon lights or that every single locker was rusty with massive holes. Just a week ago the school was in pristine condition with hardwood floor, luxurious lockers and even the air was filtered to purity.

It was all a lie and the school administration had pulled the wool over everyone's eyes including Meghan. Until now.

Last week in history class, there had been an error in the inscription that immediately broke the spell.

She had been looking at the screen one moment the next she had blinked feeling as if she had come out of a dream. She looked around the room to see all her classmates in the same broken daze. The room now looked filthy old and decaying. Her own seat was worn so thin it creaked under her. Mr. Hogan was having a panic attack screaming into his phone about children's brainwashing had worn off.

It all clicked for her then. Everything was a lie they were making her into something she didn't want to be. The perfect obedient child who was seen but never heard. She had no personality then. Now, however, she would fight back. Meghan passed a note around to everyone.

"Don't freak out, pretend you're still in a trance. Next week on Monday we take back our lives. We show them who they are messing with."

Now that she walked through the halls on the following Monday. She knew what she had to do. The riot began as soon as she walked into the classroom. Everyone raised their voices in protest. Her voice, the loudest swearing and cursing anyone who dared to do that to her. Her voice rang out against the establishment occasionally squeaking in its pubescents.

Mr. Hogan had a plan this time though. He stared at each child and listed off numbers after saying their names:

"Tiffany 87538"
"Tegan 27835"
"Brittney 56291"

Each child sat down quietly eyes glazed over in a hypnotic state. Meghan stared and yelled louder trying to get her downed classmates to rise once more; her eyes filled with panic. They continued to drop like flies until her name was called.

"Meghan 17925"

She felt something grip at her mind trying to tear it into nonexistence. She screamed in resistance though her eyes began to cloud, and numbers flashed before them. She shook her head clear.

"Meghan 17925" his voice more demanding, the numbers flashed more rapidly. She clawed at her head.

"Meghan 17925 Meghan 17925 Meghan 17925" he was panicking now, growling numbers desperately.

"NO!" she screamed loud and clear shaking her head awake permanently. She was free.

He tried to make the others go after her, but she raced out of the room. Running away from Mr. Hogan she knew her head was free. But she would have to run for the rest of her life.

Neverland

I am inspired by the tales of Peter Pan, but I always wondered what would happen if there were a bunch of lost girls. Then a beautiful dream came along and became my muse for this piece. I drew on the concept of Peter Pan, but I took it in a new different direction. ~ K.E.

Neverland was different now that Peter Pan had disappeared. The Lost Boys were now truly lost. They had also split up into two groups older kids and the younger ones. Not only that, but there were now a bunch of Lost Girls. Ever since Wendy arrived Peter realized there were many girls who needed Neverland. He started bringing girls to the island more regularly, right before he had disappeared.

Mother Wolf was the oldest girl that had been brought to Neverland and been called Mother Wolf because she took after Wendy and was a fierce warrior against the pirates. Now that there were two parties Mother Wolf stayed with the young. She looked about sixteen, but the kids loved her despite how different she was. She had come to the island with glasses and small plastic pieces in her ears. "I can't hear you without them" she would say to ensure they would not get stolen or misplaced.

Tinkerbell had spent weeks fixing them the first time they died to make sure the poor girl would have them. Pixie dust really was spectacular.

Mother Wolf sat with her knees up and her arms wrapped around them. She stared up at the night sky imagining what it would be like to be at the older kids' camp with kids her age. Neverland was great, no one ever grew up, but she felt older. She was Mother Wolf; she was responsible for the little ones. She sat there without her hearing aids for just a bit, it was her turn to relax now that most of the young ones were asleep. If they woke up, she didn't want to hear their wild screaming below in their treehouse.

She wished she could be out with the hunting parties of the older boys and girls having fun with them. She especially wished to impress Jack. He was the best hunter out of all the lost boys. Currently he was third in command at the older kid's camp, unless Peter came back, then he would go back to being fourth. Until Peter came back, they fought back and forth over the right to rule the Lost Boys.

She heard a small whining noise from behind her and let out a sigh knowing exactly what it meant. She got up slowly dusting off her skirt and leggings then put her hearing aids in one at a time. The whole world came back into loud focus.

"Mother! Mother! They sent us a letter! They want to play a game! Mother! Mother! Isn't that exciting?!" she turned to face Scamp a young boy with curly black wild hair and sparkling brown eyes almost as if they were copper pieces. He held up a willow arrow with a tattered note attached to it by twine.

Mother Wolf smiled gently leaned down and kissed his forehead. He only looked five. "I'll see what type of game they want to play all right?"

"Yes, Mother please! I want to play; they don't ever play with us." He was right. She couldn't remember the last time they all played together. It was before they realized Peter wasn't coming back. He bounced away with no dismissal. Her children were the true lost children of the world, the wild creatures that no one wanted not even the older Lost Children.

When Peter was in charge no one was left behind. She took care of everyone. She had fun and could do everything with Jack. She sighed softly and plucked the letter from the twine. Holding it to the roughly made arrow. Most likely it was Charles's arrow, a great archer but he wasn't good at crafting things. The note was small and sloppily written.

Lets play War Time
Tomorrow after lunch time
We want you to come

'That's definitely what Al and Drake would say.' Her minds-eye knew that the two boys were playing some type of trick, but she wasn't sure what kind. Her footsteps were soft as she ran gripping the wild vine of the tree sliding and swinging down to the inner most sanctum of the treehouse. As the sun had set most of the children had come into the inner most heart of the treehouse.

Now they all gathered around the center where Mother Wolf landed delicately. Their eager faces looked up in anticipation of her answer to the note. She smiled chuckled and shook her head. 'Rumors spread fast even after sleepy eyes were supposed to be in bed.'

"All right everyone." She raised her voice "We have received an invitation from the bigger kids. They would like to play wartime with us. And I think... we shouldn't go."

There were many loud disappointed sighs and whines. "But why?!" drawing out the Y at the end. "We want to play with them!" "It's not fair!" "We never have any fun!" "Please let us go!"

She knew it was a trap and someone was going to get hurt. Thirty-five children started to beg for her approval. She felt small. She could no longer hear the three that were still crying. Her head was swimming with whining insistence of the children. The high-pitched tone pounded and did not cease till finally she burst out her eyes closed. "Fine!" she screamed her body shaking but her voice gently lowered itself to a calm distraught tone. "Fine, we'll go to the game."

A scream of excitement came over them all and they danced about hollering like the wild children they were. Her knees started to shake. It was much too loud, eardrum breaking, almost. She nearly collapsed to the ground, she caught herself and slowly sat pulling her knees up to her chest again. She tried to imagine herself to be what her mother was, but she wasn't her mother. She tried not to cry and was wiping the corners of her eyes. A small hand grabbed her shoulder, behind her she saw the tear stained face of Poppy.

"I don't want to go Mother. The big kids scare me." Mother Wolf pulled Poppy into her lap gently smoothing down her hair.

"It's alright Poppy. Everything will be okay. We'll be fine." She tried to put on her big mommy voice, the one that didn't shake, the one that didn't sound scared, the one that was sure of herself. The voice of a Mother. She was a fake mother.

The next morning the kids were up at daybreak getting their toys together and painting their faces in a sloppy manner. She rushed around frantically keeping the children as calm as she could. With all the yelling she was starting to get a massive headache. She worked through it staring off into the distance occasionally. She decided to lead them down by the river near some of the downed trees and jumping rocks.

The bigger kids would find them, then the

game would begin. Wartime wasn't a fun game. There was one side against the other firing fruits and vegetables to splatter in each other's faces. For older kids it was fun, but she doubted any of her young ones would come out okay in the end. It took most of the morning to get everyone fed, dressed, and ready to go but sure enough she did it all. Then off they went following her down the path.

The area wasn't too far away that it would tire out the kids, but they were wild strong kids that had run in these woods for years. They never seemed to run out of energy. She could never remember what year it was or when the year began or ended. She had stopped counting how many times she saw the snow fairies leave or come back from the mainland. It was moment to moment in the land of never aging. They had all just gathered in the clearing with the fallen trees when the older kids jumped out screaming with ugly wooden masks on. They had spears.

Real Spears.

She turned to look at her children, but they were no longer her ducklings. They ran away from the big kids, screaming, crying, fleeing. The older kids were trying to chase them down, catch them. She saw Poppy hiding in a fallen hollow tree trunk, crying more than she had the night before. Mother Wolf tried to push her way through the chaos to get to her delicate little flower.

She stopped dead in her tracks. Her ears

rang, hissed, fizzled, then bled softly. She fell to her knee's, tears filling her eyes hands clasping her head. Someone had boxed her ears. Pawing and clawing at her ears she managed to claw the broken hearing aids out. There was now only a soft buzzing around her. Her eyes saw all the turmoil that ensued.

There were other older kids now chasing off the masked ones. Arms gently wrapped around her, standing her up gently. She looked back to see Jack holding her up. He seemed to be yelling orders to the other mask-less big kids. They were running the masked ones off and helping the little kids they could find. Jack looked at her and spoke with a concerned expression. She only heard the buzzing of the world around her. She couldn't understand him. She started to cry and hugged him. Mother Wolf didn't want to be a mother anymore.

A Touch of Poetry

Rapunzel

I have come to understand that most of my poetry takes its inspiration from a whim. This one started from a collection I decided to make about fairytales as poetry. Rapunzel was one of the first and I dedicated it to my own interpretation of the story. ~ K. E.

golden strands slide
one two three
weaves a long moment
softly sways as she
hums and stares at
shadowing mirror
brush delicate hair
decorate your head
crown of gold pins
sing louder out window
bird like song
hair weaved into a story
tossed out arched stonework
70ft tower
gold sways in wind
sways with words
wait wait
till your escape

Snow white

Another one of the fairytale collections, I tried to take on the depth of the actual story itself. However, unlike Rapunzel I decided to bring to life the idea that without the curse placed on Snow White we would not have a story. ~ K.E.

snow skin
pitch black hair
rose red lips
sing song voice
den mother
spotless small house
feed seven little men
become family
and friends
trust no one but
seven dwarves till
red apple, deaths' fruit
maiden lays still
glass case
flowers, vines grow
caress sleeping maid
No gleaming castle
No ridding off into sunsets
No prince

Without, cursed apple

I wonder (not the hymn)

This poem came from, well, wondering. Quite like my stories, poems come to me at the strangest of times though it seems poems come out of thin air. This poem was the same way. I just started to think and there it was all laid out for me. ~ K. E.

I wonder as I wander
No that's not right
I wonder as I wash my hands
I wonder staring at a blank page
I wonder walking back and forth form class
I wonder as my hands get cold while typing
I wonder staring at my betta fish
I wonder cleaning my room repeatedly
I wonder as I type assignments
I wonder lots of things
In a lot of places
But, I don't have time to wander

Art and Politics

This poem came out of an art exhibit that had its start in more of a political challenge. The exhibit came with small little descriptions underneath every picture that had some sort of political agenda. It wasn't wrong or bad, but I want a painting or an art piece to speak for itself rather than being told by the artist what I'm supposed to think.
~ K. E.

I like my art like I make my mind
open to new ideas
I don't want the buzzing News'
heads circling me like a pack of
pushy hungry Hyenas
I want to chew on the bubblegum facts
and taste the lime truth
no bobblehead candidates and violent protest
parades
'cause no one gives us the "straight and true"
I don't want to hand cuff the innocent
throw wings on the convicted!
If I want to hear about screaming left or righters
or feel like I'm a traitor for thinking
I'll flush into the infested media sewers.
I'll figure out my own opinions
THANK YOU!

Uneasy scavenger

This was inspired by a small little Coyote that I saw in West Yellowstone over my 2018-2019 Winter break from UMW. It was the only wild animal I saw that whole trip and it was coming right out of the town running, back into the forest. I could not get the image out of my head and that is the best part of poetry. To just set an image down before one's eyes and leave it alone. ~ K. E.

Dear little coyote what have you seen
    that makes you flee from this tourist town?
The engines grumble, the neon signs,
    or is it the many snowmobilers and tourists?
You trot towards the woods to your home
    glancing back over your shoulder.
Your yellow eyes scan the motels and seasonal
   houses watch the picture takers.
Lope though the snow after every glance
    your whiskers seem to twitch.
Can you find the hidden food in the locked trash-bins?
    or does someone feed you daily?
What are you thinking, little coyote?
    Do you understand the chaos in twisting roads?
Do you want to taste different Chinese foods?
    Do you know what Chinese is?
Do you want to understand these two legged creatures
    which corral together but claim "individuality"?

Or are you scared you will be followed and hunted?
    Labeled as pest or filth.
Dear little coyote, keep on running home
    lest the human beast follow to your den.

Hummingbird

My mother and grandmothers have loved hummingbirds, so we would always have a feeder out in the yard somewhere or flowers that would attract them. Often, we would find their little nests blown out of the trees and we would talk about how tiny they really were. I just had to dedicate a poem to these little creatures. ~ *K. E.*

Outside kitchen window,
flit dash
hum purr
jade, ruby, turquoise
blurred wings
zoom jitter
around feeder
gone.

Wrong way - - do not enter

My last semester of college I was asked to read a poem in front of high school poetry competition held at The University of Montana Western. This was the poem I chose to read. The title was inspired by a painted sign at an airport in a picture that I saw, it has nothing to do with the original art. I put a new life into the words and the presentation of them making this poem with the help of Japanese fish. ~ K.E.

Thoughts pass like Koi through a river
slow gleaming scales that flash
disappear into darkness
that image word Koi
bigger and flashier than all the other fish
tail flicks, fins delicate orange
loud and extravagant
you follow that Koi down
down the smooth river
don't notice
the small black Koi behind you
screaming through bubbles
"Wrong Way - - Do Not Enter"

too late
the shimmering Koi soars off
the waterfall higher than Mt. Fuji
you go with it but the little black Koi
flicks its tail and leaves you to fall
into the black depths

Midnight sessions

*This is dedicated to all those nights in college where
my assignments were so large that they required extra
work. Because this book was my senior thesis, I could not
imagine leaving this poem out. I could not have made it
through college without the fun moments, or rather hours.
~ K.E.*

Long nights
Converse over hard work
In small kitchen
Concrete lined ceiling
Linoleum floors of white
Abandoned
Dark
Welcome
No fake food or cook utensils
Small width tables
Built of plastic and metal
Long enough for everyone
When pushed together
Invite
Collaborate

Converse
Easily filled
Friends pile in
Spread out with labor
Sit next to helpers
Online and written work
Papers
Laptops
Music
Play Disney songs
Blare as we sing
"Be Prepared"
Advice unheeded
Distract from the important
Grades
Work
Insomnia
Yet we rage quit
Pour our frustrations into
Detailed heartfelt conversations
We fight back rage and sorrow
Another roadblock hit
Math
Poetry
Sex Ed
Desperate to finish
We wait till midnight
When sleep filled eyes
Exclaim enough for one day
Complete the Midnight Session

Man in a Sheppard's cap

This poem came from an encounter I had on campus as I was walking to the library. I have been told this professors name on several different occasions, but I never remember names, I remember details and faces. Honestly it made my whole day brighter after talking to this man. Thank you if you ever read this. I needed that happy bit of conversation. ~ K.E.

A peculiar day with cold weather
Never thought I'd be approached by a stranger
Weighed down by two heavy bags
I could not believe how I managed to drag
Stones of burden and of mind
My posture should have been a sign
I was walking along when he
caught my attention
A man walking in the same direction
He had on an old green Shepherds Cap
I was anxious to go inside,
my foot began to tap
But he was a nice old gentleman
With a strong coat and a nice hem
His demeanor was extraordinarily happy

Said the luggage looked heavy
Asked what was my major
English, I said to him curious
about his behavior
He spoke to me of a high school teacher
Which was the only one he could remember
She was there to teach English
He was so distinguished
What an interesting thing to say
Especially to someone you
just met along your way
His demeanor was cheery
Despite the day being so utterly dreary
Then away he went with his salvation
No hand did he lend though his
words seemed like fiction
He made my day brighter in
that small conversation
The old man and his words
and his kind disposition

Glendive playground

This happens to be one of my fondest memories as a little girl. I don't know how old I was, but I never forgot this playground. It was such a happy memory and I don't ever want to let it go. Special moments like this need to be memorialized, which is why I wrote this poem. ~ K.E.

The long green neck stands
tall; a small girl
stares up at the beast.
Cattails rise like sunflowers,
raise leaves to meet the reptile.
The green beast doesn't move;
can't get up without help.
The see-saw more fun
rides up and down
with a father.
The merry-go-round spins with the wind.
The girl ignores the dino once more
rushes to the twirl of the metal.
Mother pushes her feet off.
Swing and watch Father and child.
Father insists once,

placing the girl upon the neck of
the green statue.
With father's help she sits
a rider atop a horse,
but soon swings
entertain the girl.
But the pictures are fuzzy.
Was this what happened?
Memory fades
Pictures gone
The long green neck stands
tall; casts it's shadow over
the family.

As high as birds

I found that whenever I was in a classroom my mind would wander even if it was for just a moment. While I was sitting in my first poetry class, I happened to look out the window of the English Seminar room into the large pine tree. There they were, a few doves hopping around on the branches and flying out of the tree. Daydreaming can be the best inspiration sometimes. ~ K.E.

Top of the trees covered with cones
The other limbs bare
Trees five stories high
Branches not strong enough to climb,
But birds fly high to the top,
Raising their young
They can see everything
Through the seeds that never fall.

Such a height is terrifying to those
Who cannot fly
But why oh why
Is it so magnificent to imagine?

If only once I could see

From the top of the trees
Feet on one branch
Hand over my forehead
Peer out into the world
See everything.

All the people the places around
If only I could never look straight down
But I can not
So I will sit watch
The birds out the window.

Seamstress

I love to sew costumes, though currently, I am still a beginner. When I was writing this, I was in UMW's costume shop for the theatre. I thought about the sewing machine, the skills required to make good clothing, and my family members such as my grandmother and mother. Art, even in a practical sense such as sewing, has a heart to it that one can just feel. ~ K.E.

A sound of concentration and the fast pace of the beating of the needle on fabric. A silent sound of wants and accomplishments.

How eerie the thump thump thump can be when knowing the diligent seamstress pours her heart out onto the fabric, in colors that bleed into the seams, like paint. Such a hard task. Laboring away.

No one knows the pain of heart beats. No one can hear the throb of the machine and the body. No one but the seamstress.

Upcoming Books

World of wolf

This world is corrupt. The earth once known to inhabit humans and mythical creatures is now in chaos. The myths once seen as fictive ideas roam the world controlling it with disaster. Though it is no longer the humans' world, they are not the only ones persecuted. The world had a great war when mighty legends decided they themselves wanted to rule. The war raged on for 50 years. The Dragons, Were-people, Vampires, and Humans all fought for the same thing. The Dragons were the first to fall. Though their power was great they were few in number and were known to fight battles on their own for they could not stand the sight of each other for more than a day. Some who saw the mighty Dragons as an asset tried to recruit the creatures but could not gain their trust. The Dragons who weren't slaughtered went into hiding as they had done long before magic came back to the earth.

The Were-people were the next to fall out of the world's graces. Their main goal was to bring balance to the world. The narrow-minded Vampires refused to make this a possibility. The Weres' and the Vampires were already ancient enemies, and both were passionate creatures. The Vampires brutally killed off the Weres' losing many of their own in the process. The Were-council sought a union to defeat the blood sucking monsters. They surmised that fighting with the humans was their only option of world peace. Humans had the numbers and were fed up with seeing their brothers and sisters being used as food for the Vampires.

For many years the two forces joined together, fighting side by side. But the Humans would often label anything that was not them or part of the once existing world as a diabolical threat. Fights and massacres would often break out amongst the ranks and more Weres' were lost. The fighting population for the Weres' dwindled and soon the humans put them as second-class fighters sending the creatures out first just so they would be slaughtered. The Weres' saw this and retaliated turning on the humans. They tried to fight both enemies. This is what led to their demise.

Once the Weres' lost the humans were helpless and died very quickly without the aid of "magic". Human soldiers would become Vampire feasts if they were captured. Thus, the war ended quickly to spare the lives of the humans. They surrendered their fruitless efforts and tried to reason with the new rulers. The humans were tricked into thinking they would become second class citizens and would have at least an idyllic life.

That was an optimistic idea. After only 3 months the Vampires decided it wasn't worth it to keep up the facade. They treated the humans as their personal food slaves unlike the other creatures that had just been thrown out to be common day rabble. The earth's population was a mix of humans and lesser creatures. The Vampires ruled from then on. They ruled with iron fists. They treated everything under them as scum. The Weres' on the other hand seemed to disappear from existence. They hid despising the humans for their treachery and hating the vampires the same as they did before. The few that were still around became egregious people. The creatures would be reported to the guards, known to be foul smelling creatures like Orcs and Goblins, and were either slaughtered on the spot or were taken to the head vampires of the city to be publicly executed. This is how life was for the past hundred years. One hundred years is to long though for such misery to edure.

Chapter 1: Enemies of the wolf
A figure draped in a long flowing black

hooded trench coat absconded down the street covering its face. The rain drenched the people who were bustling about trying to take shelter. If one looked close enough at the faces and features of the people, one would see they were not all human. The fairies already hid within every aperture that was dry. The other larger creatures such as humans, half humans, and orcs all pushed their ways into stores or rushed to their homes.

The creature in the black trench coat did no such thing. It hurried quickly into the alleyways wrapping its cloak tighter to itself. The creature smirked as it walked, pleased at its good fortune of the rain pouring down at this point in the day. It would begin its long journey out of the city. The big drapery would not stick out at all compared to if it had worn such a garment in the sunlight. The back streets were almost completely empty except for a few hoboes that lined the dumpster bins. It was easy to find its way out of the city and into the hidden pathways of the forest. Once within the denseness of the foliage it ran fast. It was faster than any human and now that it was out of the disastrous city it nearly danced along with excitement. It ran desiring to get to the ancient ruins where the covert meeting was to take place.

As it ran it shed its mighty coat draping it over its shoulder. The lack of over wear revealed a muscular woman with an air of a wildness about her. Her dark black hair and blue eyes stood out against her light pale pinkish skin tone. She ran through the forest with an elegance and understanding one would only obtain if they had lived in the forest all their lives. She was happy, for the first time in two weeks she was in her natural surroundings. The city never pleased her. It was a ruined place compared to the old villages that used to be scattered amongst the British Isles.

Though she had not lived back then she had read about what the world was like before the Great War. She had always looked back at the stories and thought about what the author was going through when he or she had chronicled the account. She could almost imagine the world before. She could practically see it before her eyes. That old world had had its own flaws, destruction and death. It led her to this life which she knew nothing more than to hide in the shadows.

When she realized she was fantasizing again; she shook her head and slowed her pace. She smelt the air as she got closer to the ruins. She could smell the sentry hiding in the shadows waiting for her. She slowed enough to go into a nobler stance. His back straightened, and her chin rose. Her words were clear and soft so that it would not raise too much of an alarm. The sentry was still hidden within the concealed look out post he watched intently with bright golden eyes.

"The woods are dangerous for a young vampire. But since you are already here why don't we enjoy a snack?" This was a stanza from one of the vampire fairytales. It was a play on the human's old Little Red Riding Hood story. Instead of all the good characters being human they were vampires. The villain of the story was still the same. The great wolf waited to eat the little girl up. The story was usually told to young vampires so they would stay away from odd looking strangers and it was also a way to promote the vampires being the ultimate good.

The sentry nodded as he heard the signal phrase. He gave a low huff that half sounded like a laugh and a growl, indicating she could come inside. The sentence always made him smile. The Were-people had used the two lines as a cryptic phrase to let the ones who knew it into the few strongholds the people had. It was a mockery of the story and almost everyone old enough to understand thought it very clever and an enjoyable phrase.

The black-haired girl walked forward through the large crumbling doorway. The guard came out and greeted her in his half creature form. His human like figure looked strong and even more aggressive with the fur, tail, and head of the wolf.

The mighty Were-wolf sentry's assets where mostly based on his strength and size. He was one of the largest of all the wolves in this area. His dark blackish brown fur was covered with black leather armor with hints of red trailing along the edges and the details. If one stood back the armor did hide his many scars, scars he had gotten in service of his people. The black-haired girl knew him almost too well. He was her older brother after all. She could tell where every scar ended and started since she was the one who fixed him up the most. They were both very protective of each other and as they stood there in the dark ruin of a hallway. All they could do was stand and stare into each other's eyes smiling happily.

She had been gone far too long for his approval. He had worried about her the entire time. She like him did the same. They were the only two left from their family's pack and didn't want to lose each other. But the council demanded a lot from them. He was the best guard because he had the best judicious mind in the whole fighting class. She could easily disguise herself and collect information in the large cities and none of the blood suckers or their pets would have ever known she had come and gone. This constantly led to their long separations, that normally lasted for many weeks.

They clasped each other's arms in a friendly way. She hugged him remembering how close she was to never seeing him again. He embraced her openly not without consciousness that she must have gotten into some form of trouble within the city. His body stiffened as his ears picked up a small sound from outside the ruins. His now morose mood turned even worse as he pushed his sister to the side and behind a wall. He quickly and quietly went back to his post. The smell of this noise was unfamiliar.

The artifice that approached the ruins was well planned out. The man was dressed in thick red leather armor. His eyes were a bright electric blue just like the sister. His dark black hair fell around his face almost framing it. The skin that showed was a light tannish and could be compared to that of a working man out in the fields of the old Irish meadows. He may have seemed attractive to the sister, but he had so many different perfumes and colognes on it nearly sent the brother and sister into vomiting fits. The Weres' had some of the most sensitive noses in the entire world and this smell was disgusting beyond belief. They both kept themselves composed despite their immense need to be sick. The brother kept his eyes on the stranger who approached the ruins slowly.

The outsider smiled despite his disgusting smell. The sister hunched herself over in a ball quietly so her stomach wouldn't turnover anymore. 'How on earth can this man stand the scent that his own body puts off? He must know, it is too potent for even a human to ignore.' His wretched smell did not distract the brother from his salutation though. It was the same words his sister had just spoken. The new arrival walked forward into the ruins.

The smell got worse and worse the sister shook viciously trying to keep herself from being ill. The brother stood ignoring all his discomfort. Slowly unsheathed his mighty sword and waited.

The stranger sniffed the air as if he could actually smell anything beyond the stench. His eyes darted around slowly as he walked forward. He soon saw the sister. He spoke softly with an inimitable voice that resembled a kind young ruler.

"Are you not used to disguising you're scent she wolf?" she looked up through blurry eyes. Her brother quickly jumped out swinging his long-sword down on the intruder. But to his surprise the trespasser caught the attack with his own clay-more. He attacked quickly and with much power and the brother was caught fighting on the defen-sive. He tried to emulate the moves of the stranger but began to falter. The red armored man quickly hit his opponent and knocked him to the ground his body slumped over in unconsciousness state.

"Randall!" she screamed out to her brother whose inert body slouched against an old cracked column. She tried to force herself to get up and protect her brother, but her body failed her. The stranger walked over to her weak body. He crouched down to look her in the eyes.

"Your brother is fine she-wolf. He will just have a bump on his head. He did attack me after all." He stretched out his hand to lay it upon her shoulder but she coward away as best she could. Her head pulsed with the pain the stench was causing. "Easy now, it's okay, I won't hurt you." His voice soothed the immense pounding that drowned out almost everything she could possibly do to think and say. He caught her before she fell to the ground unconscious.

The stranger thought to himself. 'Have I disguised myself too well?' He had gotten used to his own smell and had all but forgotten that it was too strong. He listened to the shallow breathing of the two fallen wolves. His ears perked as he heard the trickling of water. He steadied the girl then went and pulled the mighty male back into his sentry's post to hide him. He went back to the girl who groaned and shook even in her comatose state.

He slowly picked her up and realized something had dropped out of her pocket. He reached down still cradling her and looked to find that it was an ancient locket. It was well cared for but worn heavily by time. Quickly he looped it around his sword so as not to lose it. He looked down to her face which twisted in pain. He sighed and carried her towards the sound that he had heard.

He quickly found the water in a room. It was a large area with a pool of clear greenish water in the center. He decided this must be where the sentry's stay while on their watch for there were several bed rolls and a few storage containers. He couldn't understand why there was only one sentry now. She was obviously not one of the guards. The water was dripping off of large boulders that had fallen in through the ceiling and into the pool which was big enough to seat five people comfortable. He laid the girl down on a bed roll lightly, as to not wake her. His resignation for a bath became clearer as he watched her curl up tighter around her stomach. Taking his sword off, he laid it beside her then quickly submerged himself fully clothed and armored into the water. This was dystopian idea for him as he sank into the water with a splash. His armor weighed him down and made it horribly difficult to scrub away the nuisance of the smell. He didn't know why but he wanted her to feel at peace around him. The smell needed to go immediately. He glanced at her distressed composure.

He shook his head violently with caprice. 'No, I must not think of anything but my mission. Besides if the sentry acted with disdain to my smell so will the council. It's not just her displeasure I'm concerned about.' He growled as he thought of her reaction to him. He could almost picture her cowering away from him once more. She wasn't a submissive wolf, he sensed that. He knew it deep down within his blood. It made him angry that he had done that to such a powerful wolf. He looked at her again. 'Why did it affect you more than your brother though?' The smell of the vampires' city still lingered on her and he knew she had been used to horrible smells. He tried to count how many scents he had used. 'Ten, fifteen, twenty?' he counted 25 different fragrances he had used to disguise himself. He dunked his head under water and ran his hands through his hair wanting desperately to subdue the ferocious odor of his disguise.

He heard movement through the water and

quickly jerked himself up gasping as he felt the new air. He froze when he felt the tip of his claymore pressed lightly to his neck. "Don't move you scum, or I will not hesitate to let this pool fill with your blood." He blinked away the water that fell into his eyes and looked up at the she-wolf. He resented the nickname she had given him. 'Scum?! Can't you see I did this for you?!' he blinked in shock from the quick attack but also at this insignificant thought.

"I have done you no ill will on purpose shewolf." He raised his hands slowly. His dialogue surprised her slightly. She was only called she wolf by the ones who outranked her, and there weren't many.

"You have attacked my brother! You have no right to say you have done me no ill will!" She growled with a sharpness that would match that of an alpha. 'This is the way you should act.' His reserved thought did not distract him from the fact that she had his sword to his throat.

"I am sorry she-wolf, but he did attack me even when I had spoken the secret phrase." He let this sink in for a minute then speedily grabbed his claymore and pulled it away from her, his gloves protecting him from the sharp bite of the edge. Caught off guard she fell into the pool. Once she was in the water, he laughed softly but she had fallen into a state of utter panic. She burst to the surface coughing up the water she accidentally swallowed. He saw her struggling and helped her,pulling her close so she could use him as a stabilizer and get her bearing. She started to bark out curses in the old wolf language making a vociferous attempt to let him know he'd wronged her.

"You know old wolf?" He asked ignoring her verbiage. She growled sharply still coughing.

"Of course I do, you arrogant half mauled rotten carcass!" she barked out wiping water out of her eyes. He couldn't help but to laugh at her insult. He had never heard it spoken in the human's common tongue; the language most used in the world. It sounded so much less threatening than it would have if she had spoken it in the old language, like she did a minute ago. She felt the heat rush to her face and let her anger and embarrassment take over. She slammed herself into him knocking him off balance. She didn't realize till it was too late that he had grabbed her arm. They both fell into the deeper part of the pool with a huge splash.

Caught off balance he struggled not to drown. His armor weighed him down. He hadn't realized he had grabbed her until he felt her squirming around above him. She kneed him but he felt her jerk as she must have caught a sharp edge of his armor. She struggled more as they both sunk to the bottom of the deep end of the pool. He pushed her up with his arms forcing her towards the surface. He watched her float up and turned his body abruptly so he could push off the bottom with his legs and hands. It was strange to him that this pool could be twelve feet deep. He came to the surface again gasping for air.

She was struggling to keep herself afloat. She had always hated the deep waters it made her feel like she was trapped. She had realized it was wrong of her to struggle so much because now she was almost out of energy. It felt like her strength leaked out into the water. She didn't move from where she was floating even though she heard the stranger. Despite dragging her down with him, he had forced her up.

He looked at her form as they both breathed heavily. He grabbed her waist lightly as he noticed her growing weak. Neither said a word as they slowly swam back to the shallow end of the pool. He only stole glances at her, mad at himself for grabbing this she-wolf he hardly knew. This was no time to act like a pup. Her eyes were glazed over with darkness as if she had just seen an entire pack slaughtered by vampires. 'Is she really that afraid of deep water?' He questioned. But he knew that conclusion was wrong. It wasn't just fear it seemed more than that. Was it him? Did he do this?

"I'm sorry I didn't mean for that to happen. Are you alright she-wolf?" He didn't loosen his grip and she was somewhat grateful for the touch of a living being. She realized he had made her feel safe with this one gesture and she wanted to smack herself for thinking such things about an outsider especially one who had attacked her brother and had nearly drown her twice. It was a bit of an exaggeration, but she didn't care.

"I'm fine now ... But you're barking mad if you think pulling me in with you would have solved anything!" She yelled pushing him away and crossing her arms. Her face once a deathly white turned bright red. He laughed lightly in pure happiness. 'Her spirit is back.'

***

Randall woke up completely groggy. At first, he could not discern where he was. His nose scrunched continuously. His obstinate senses refused to readjust and focus. 'What happened?' He couldn't quite remember, his head hurt, and he was getting even more irritated. Then the influx of memories hit him with a force like a great Grizzly Bear Were. He scrambled up on his feet with a fierce anger. 'Annora! My Sister!' He looked around frantically trying to find her. He growled harshly forcing his dizzy body to go forward. He sensed something and looked to see the aged face of the chieftain.

The old grey Wolf stood a head taller than him and was much larger in general. His power seemed to resonate in the very air he breathed.

"Hush Randall. Who attacked you?" Randall growled and looked down he was anxious to find his sister. He felt her presence somewhere in this ruin. A sharp sting struck the tip of his ear and he realized he had hesitated to long.

"Sorry Sir. There was an intruder. He was suspicious and he fought back. He knocked me out and my sister's gone." Randall's eyes kept darting around the room looking for a sign of his sister and the intruder's whereabouts. He needed a way to implicate that mongrel to this situation or else the Chieftain would lose faith in him.

The Old Wolf looked at the younger black one. He didn't think the boy's story was quite so ludicrous. The air still had the light stench of something he couldn't put a distinct name too. Randall was jittery and excited waiting to find Annora. His muscles twitched with the urgency to run and track. The Chieftain sympathized with the young wolf. He had known much death and now the horror of his sister's disappearance was a completely abstruse idea. The Chief knew all too well that he couldn't restrict the poor wolf any longer.

"Botolf take Randall's position. Watch for any more intruders." He barked over his shoulder to a much younger wolf who just nodded sharply before taking up the post. "Randall come, let us find your sister and that intruder." At those words Randall was now an irrepressible force. He jolted down the corridors and hallways speedily following the fading scent. The Chieftain jogged not really caring if he could catch up with the younger wolf.

Randall stopped short within a corridor. His mind nearly stopped looking at the inexplicable scene before him. The Chieftain caught up with him and investigated the sentry's barracks. Annora stopped herself in the middle of a long stream of wolf curses that were directed at the stranger who laughed, smiling in amusement. She looked at her brother and screamed out in happiness. "Randall!" She jumped out of the water trying to run to her brother but slid around more than anything. She threw herself into her brother's arms.

Randall held Annora close wrapping his strong furry arms around her protectively. He looked at the stranger and growled sharply. The intruder had a more duplicitous plan than Randall had originally thought. The mongrel wanted his sister. The Chieftain pushed forward into the room looking the man straight in the eyes.

"Convel looks like you're up to your old ways again, making trouble for me as always." He went to the water's edge extending his arm for the lone wolf. Convel took it gratefully knowing he could not manage to get out of the pool without help.

"Ullok old friend, I haven't done anything too troubling. Besides those days are long over. I'm no longer a pup remember." He gave the Chieftain a quirky smile that said otherwise.

"Everyone's a pup to me." The Chieftain laughed.

"That's because you're an old testy bur." He shook his wet armor lightly once he was on dry ground.

"You know that bashed brain lunatic?!" Annora growled looking to her chieftain.

Hunted

This tale started with my interest in the steampunk community. My mind was full heartedly in a Steampunk universe when I wrote this though I did not give as much detail about the culture as I had intended. Later when I make it into its own novel I will add more details and show the interesting aspects of these characters in that type of setting. ~ K.E.

Before she knew what happened she was alone in a dark room. "I know you're here" she said quietly. She turned in a full circle till she faced forward again. A blade cut across her eye. She stumbled back clutching the area trying to hold back the blood that pooled in her hand. Her good eye locked with his and he was much too close to her with the knife that was in his hands. She pointed her pistol at him her sight blurring with the pain. "Surrender now Chauncey."

"Surrender? Why would I do that?" He smiled like the devil. "No, no, you see my dear that wouldn't work. There's only death waiting for me back there." He moved closer. She backed up a step and fired, missed.

"Stay there! That was a warning shot. I will kill you where you stand." He paid no attention to her and moved forward in a quick motion, slapping the gun from her hand and slamming her into the wall behind her.

"If you were going to shoot me you shouldn't have hesitated." Laughter hung on his tongue. She never looked away from him which made him excited and upset. He would dominate her and teach her the place that she belonged. She was no longer the hunter she was now the prey.

She flung her bloody hand at his face to keep him back, but he caught her wrist holding it gently while forcing her against the wall with half his strength. Gently he licked the blood off her fingertips.

"I will make you bleed little woman. None of your comrades will be able to save you. They will come looking for me, after they see you, I will destroy them one by one. Then you will know this is your fault for stepping out of your place." He slid a knife down her left arm and shoved his knee into her gut.

Randal Wilkins and the four Lieutenants struggled with their entrapments cursing the foul monster who had set them. Chauncey new his target and his prey. It was hard to stop General Lenora Elmstone when she was so close to her prey, but Randal had been hunting the monster much longer. If only she would have listened. He knew something was wrong. He cut the last of the ropes and looked at her men.

"We haven't heard any gun shots, maybe she hasn't found him" Bentley Pankhurst, the youngest lieutenant said just as a gun went off. They began to speed down the corridors.

"He wanted her to come after him. He wanted only her." Randal slowed as he noticed a few more traps that were ready to be triggered. He motioned towards them and tried to find a path where none would be tripped.

"With how slow we're going she's in a whole lot of trouble." Zadock Fielding shot at the pommel that swung towards the group when a pressure plate was stepped on.

"Can't believe none of you have faith in General Elmstone. She's not stupid enough to just let herself die." They all glanced back at Horiace Hogwood. "You all underestimate her. She didn't become General by just doing paperwork. She's fought hard and long in the Lector War. Not once did she give in." He slung his riffle over his shoulder and pulled out the revolver.

"Even if she's good, Chauncey doesn't care. She's a woman in power and to him that's all he needs to know in order to torture her. He's done it to thousands so far... many of them were soldiers in the Lector War. He wants them to struggle and fight till he can force them to submit to him. He thinks that will make them submit to all men. He thinks he is fixing a problem." Randal slowed as they came to another doorway. The ruins were caked with odd corridors and rooms. It was mazelike.

"We can't lose another General not on our watch" Rodrick Bagstock whispered clutching an old shot gun with rage.

They cleared the next room triggering none of the traps Chauncey had laid. Rowland knew that this was what Chauncey did to slow his hunters down. All the traps were set and ready but being so cautious with every step made them linger far too long. The screaming started much later than he expected. Either Chauncey didn't start his fun right away or she was strong just as her lieutenant had said.

Her screams seemed to come from everywhere at first, all four lieutenants going mad at the sound. Randal stayed quiet and slowly started leading them down into the depths of what might have been a dungeon at one point. The screams didn't stop for a half an hour at least. He knew they were too slow.

The sounds of pain stopped abruptly and then there was nothing but silence. Down here there were no traps. The men stayed quiet and cautious.

"This is Chauncey's chosen play area. He might still be down here so keep your guard up. Though if the record stands, we will find her before we find his tracks." growled Randal taking his own rifle out getting ready for the hunt. "With such big prey Chauncey might stay around to see his victims rescued."

They cleared each cell and hall that they came across. Down here it was nicely lit by torches, to help them search. As they came to one of the larger hallways, they heard soft breathing and small noises. It seemed to echo against the rocks.

"Rats?"

Randal shook his head "No, human."

They all crept slowly once more clearing each room until they came to the last cell, closed off by a wooden door. The noises seemed to dominate the room beyond it. Randal pushed the creaky door open his weapon raised, cautious about what was in there. What they saw they hated. General Lenora Elmstone lay tied to a bed fallen in due to its age and her weight. Her clothes were torn and shredded in some parts. Blood dripped from a slice across her eye and a place that looked like it was somewhere beyond her hair. The light seeped in through the door barely illuminating her.

Bentley rushed to her, started to wipe her face, put pressure on her forehead, and tried to untie her hurriedly. She didn't seem to notice. "General, hey we're here now everything will be alright." He leaned her against him, her right side shifted into the light more. She didn't seem to comprehend or focus. Her eyes glazed over in a daze. Her breathing was shallow. Randal looked towards the others.

"He might still be here hurry let's try to figure out where he went." Randal looked back at her and gently kneeled down. "Can you speak?" her eyes didn't focus on him, didn't focus on anything. The others rushed to find the criminal or his escape route.

"What's wrong with her? Did he hit her head that hard? There isn't any blood coming out of her ears so she can hear." Bentley held her to him with one hand pressed tightly against her head.

"I suspect not ... I think maybe this is just a phase of shock or something like her blocking things out to protect herself. Could be a bit of blood loss."

The three men rushed back. Zadock looked a bit disgruntled and spoke first "I found where he would have gone to escape. It's a clear path to the surface." He looked ready to kill and Randal didn't doubt that he would.

"Everywhere else seems clear down here so he must have run unless there are some hidden paths." Horiace said gruffly.

"Let's go get him then we know which way he's going. He's gotta pay for this and all that he's done" Zadock turned tense and ready to attack.

Bentley looked up and growled "No we have to get her out of here. She might get worse if she stays down here for too long."

"We can't let him do this to anyone else and if he escapes, he will. The General might have hurt him which will slow him down. He might be smart, but if he's injured there isn't a whole lot he can do." Rodrick offered.

"You all can stay but I'm going to hunt him down and drag him back beaten." Zadock left with grunt, Rodrick nodded and followed him. Horiace stepped out of the way and watched them go.

"We shouldn't split up to hunt him. Don't leave your general!" Randal yelled at them standing again. She seemed to understand what he said and tried to speak but shook, coughing a bit instead.

"Bugger off Bounty Hunter!" Zadock yelled from down the hall. They were gone and Horiace let out a groan.

"They would have never done this to our old General."

Bentley cooed softly to Elmstone "Easy there general we have you. They are being idiots but we'll protect you."

She looked up to everyone in the room still not seeing straight. "Yyou got yourselves free?" She leaned back against Bentley. The question seemed like it was asked in a dream, like she thought that it wasn't real and had hardly any hope.

"He did this to you didn't he." It was more of a statement but meant to get her back on track. Randal gently caressed the fresh cut going from just above her eyebrow to her lower cheek. The initial cut wasn't deep or else it would have taken her eye, but it seemed that he went back and made it deeper so that the scar would last longer.

"You'll be able to see better when it stops hurting, your visions probably blurry from the pain. Where else did he hurt you Lenora?"

"We have to stop the bleeding from her head. It doesn't seem to be clotting very well" Bentley looked at Randal concerned holding her tighter to him nervous that the bounty hunter would take off on the hunt as well.

"Here" Horiace ripped a piece of his under shirt, which was thick and long, handing it over to Bentley. It could wrap around her head two times with a bit of pressure to slow the bleeding. She seemed to be a bit more conscious when the binding was tied.

"I am fine." she stuttered.

"Like hell you are. Now where all does it hurt?" Randal gently started to move her scrapped clothing to see if he could see anymore. Her right hand shot up to slap him with surprising amount of power, but she was a bit too slow. Randal caught it. His grip was slick, and he growled turning her arm over to reveal another long gash from just above her elbow all the way down to her wrist. She looked as if she was being drained of life as he began to realize all the damage. Her left leg was definitely broken, she had bruises that were forming in the spots he could see around her ribs, not to mention the ones forming on her wrists, neck and anywhere that seemed like it would be visible in a mirror. He was almost sure her back was decently untouched.

She seemed to fade the more he looked at her till her eyelids fluttered to a complete close. Her breathing was stable though, so her lungs weren't punctured. He assumed the earlier coughing was her trying to get her breath back after the choke hold.

Bentley whispered softly trying to hold her like a brother would. "The general won't be pleased with them."

"She'll be furious" Horiace mumbled as Bentley tried to pick her up as gently as he could but she flinched even in her unconscious state it was as if her body had already gained the muscle memory of an abused dog. He looked hurt and upset at the reaction as if it was an insult to.

"Don't worry I'll get her" Randal gently leaned down and picked her up unperturbed when she flinched. "Let's get her out of here." They followed Horiace out towards the new exit though it was difficult to get her up and above ground. All of them were on guard from then on.

Forgotten life

I have plans for this one, but I have to organize all the ideas before I truly start to write more. This will be the beginning of a story that's core concept is amnesia, which I have a hard time writing. I don't want it to seem fake or like some poorly written fan fic. I have experience writing those too. For my readers however I want to present something better. ~ K. E.

I walked slowly through the damp foliage. The forest was quiet which my delicate footsteps did not disturb. My heart, though loud in my mind, thumped silently in my chest, fast, hard. My breathing was as silent as my heart and matched the pace of it. I couldn't remember why I was so anxious. My eyes widened as realization hit me 'I don't remember anything.' I could only picture the reality of the times. Castles, kings, knights, peasants, magic. I counted them out on my fingers holding them up and letting the numbers sink in.

"What about my past?" I mumbled staring at my toes.

"What about it?" A gravely male voice answered. I spun around to meet the stranger. I unsheathed my short sword with an automatic reflex I didn't know I had. The man hid in the shadows of two large Elder trees. His cloak was only a few shades darker than the shadows that concealed the upper part of his face. His well-muscled body seemed controlled even though he was half leaning on the Elder to the left. He wore no armor besides his leather gauntlets. His cloak draped over his shoulders and revealed a loose shirt of dark green. He seemed to look like a hunter more than anything else. His boots were well broken in, I guessed from tracking his prey. But this hunter was different he had a sword fastened to his waist with a black leather belt to accompany his bow and arrows.

"Are you going to attack me or not?" I mumbled. He shook his head and folded his arms. His smile crept across his lips in a mocking manner. I lowered my short sword and eyed him curiously.

"Did you find something you like?" He chuckled.

I stepped back into the woods grumbling my annoyance "Leave me alone. I don't know you and there's no reason why you should come near me." I started to circle him ready to leave the area. I didn't know where I wanted to go but being here with him was unsafe. He just watched as I circled and when I bolted, he stayed behind.

Quite a ways off I slowed and took a breath. I looked around; nothing was familiar. "What even is my name?" I kept looking at the ground hoping that the memory would come from the warm strong earth. I kept walking not looking, trying to remember anything, anything at all. Then he was there in front of me once more and I never heard him. I unsheathed a dagger I had hidden on my waist.

"I've never seen you show that dagger to anyone but your trusted friends. You don't remember me, but have you really forgotten everything else?" The stranger leaned against another tree and watched me. He looked at the dagger more. Anger flowed through me like it was my blood. I didn't want him to look at it. I sheathed it back in its place.

He stared at me, he seemed to be searching for something. Not on me but in me somewhere something deep and hidden. I didn't know what it was. He knew, he definately knew what I was in my past. He knew everything about me. It seemed to be an eternity before I realized this stranger was hugging me. I blinked in shock and stared at the back of his neck and his soft hair.

"L-leave me alone!" I screamed and tried to push him away, his grip was a bit too strong.

"You don't remember me? Not even now?" His words turned into a soft growl and his grip tightened. "Don't you remember the battle, the escape? I told you to run I thought this was one of your games. You were where we were supposed to meet so I thought maybe, maybe you were playing a game." He pulled away and shook me by the shoulders even when I tried to get free I couldn't. He stared at me as if he hadn't noticed my struggling. "You were supposed to be fine that's what the escape plan meant. Why aren't you alright? Why can't you remember me?"

He looked distraught and all I could do was stare at him. I didn't know him; I didn't know anything about this. I don't even know myself.

Made in the USA
Middletown, DE
12 February 2024